WAR OF THE IMMORTALS

ALSO BY BRENT TOWNS

WAR OF THE IMMORTALS

THE GODS OF WAR
BOOK 6

BRENT TOWNS

ROUGH
EDGES
PRESS

War of the Immortals
Paperback Edition
Copyright © 2024 Brent Towns

Rough Edges Press
An Imprint of Wolfpack Publishing
1707 E. Diana Street
Tampa, FL 33610

roughedgespress.com

Paperback ISBN 978-1-68549-737-8
eBook ISBN 978-1-68549-619-7
LCCN 2024950167

WAR OF THE IMMORTALS

MI6 INTERROGATION SITE, LONDON

This was it. The ultimate day of the inquiry/ interrogation/ probe that had so far spanned five days, which somehow felt like five months. My name is John Reaper Kane. Reaper after the Grim Reaper tattoo on my back. Beside me—like a never-ending encore—were Holly Smith and Raymond Knocker Jensen. Our close-knit, seasoned team was well-versed in what was to come, and our experiences on this series of missions had pushed us to the limit physically and mentally. Now we had to justify our battlefield actions to a group of bureaucrats one last time.

Holly and Knocker were Brits, and I consider them both friends. Knocker and I had many physical similarities: height and build, roughly the same age, unshaven—his beard, like his hair, was a little lighter than mine—and we were both former military men. He was SAS, I was Recon Marine. Holly, on the other hand, was a shade under six feet, had short blonde hair and a button nose. An experienced MI6 operative, she had been our handler for the fight against the Russian generals known as The Gods of War.

I am pleased to point out that at this juncture, some of

*them had gone to meet their gods. Now, as far as the debrief
was concerned, that number stood at two.*

*Seated at the familiar conference table, we now awaited
the arrival of our interrogation panel. At the outset of
proceedings all those days ago, the environment had been
much less hospitable, a small, stark, and sterile interrogation room. I was grateful we had graduated to something
larger and a little more comfortable.*

*Basically, the hearings were a farce. We were endeav-
oring to flush out a mole named Hecate. This was the final
question mark over the whole mission, which had
commenced in Syria, going on to span the globe.*

*In that time, we had lost friends and colleagues, gone
but not forgotten. We had also thwarted some grand but
nefarious schemes along the way. Our biggest prize so far,
Sergey Lash, the former president of the new USSR. After
some determined interrogation, he had come around to our
way of thinking and agreed to talk. There was, however, a
price. One I was compelled to carry out once the proceedings
were concluded.*

*When the most propitious time presented itself, we
would produce him, setting him in play. Until that point we
would carry out our charade through to the end.*

"This is it," I whispered out of the corner of my mouth.

*"Thank God for that," Knocker replied, a little bleary-
eyed.*

I stared at him. "Did you get much sleep last night?"

*"A little," he replied with a straight face. "About the
same amount as the new PM."*

"For crying out loud," Holly groaned.

"Wasn't my fault," he replied.

I might just stop here and explain that the UK's new

Prime Minister is the ex-wife of our illustrious friend. "You obviously didn't learn from past mistakes."

"Shit, Reaper, I'm not marrying her."

Movement to our right drew our attention and we scrutinized the three people who filed in. Charles German, Jack Holland, and Christine Ryan. Each was a forty-something politician, Ryan having been MI6 before her foray into the base world of politics. Both men were attired in their standard black suits. Christine Ryan, like a rose between two thorns, lit up the room with her emerald-green dress, somewhat anomalous from her customary apparel.

The three took up their positions opposite us and prepared the folders they'd brought with them. Looking up at us, German said, "Good morning. How are we all today?"

We muttered a few words, and German said, "All rearing to go, I see."

He looked down at his papers and said, "It seems we're up to where you finally commit to an operation concerning General Shatov, General Morozov, and something called Hephaestus. Would that be correct?"

Holly nodded. "It would."

"Then we should get started."

I stared at them across from me. This was it. Today was the day, the culmination of the previous five. It was time.

SON OF THE GODS

HEPHAESTUS, THE SON OF ZEUS AND HERA, WAS SAID TO be the God of metalworking, artisans, metallurgy, carpenters, forges, sculpting, and blacksmiths, along with being a member of the Twelve Olympians. But in this case, Hephaestus was the God of fire and volcanoes: all things destructive.

Built in Volgograd between 1975 and 1977, it was the realized idea of the early generals. It was the backup to their plan. Should things go awry, then Hephaestus could be unleashed on Europe. The city of Paris was selected as the ideal position.

Known as a super nuke, Hephaestus was designed to do as much damage as possible while spreading maximum radiation. The detonation was intended to add a defensive barrier between East and West.

The designer, a scientist named Franz Vogts, was an East German recruited by the Russian nuclear program. From there, he had been taken aside and asked to design something big for the generals.

Although reluctant at first, he was finally persuaded and convinced to do their bidding.

It took Vogts two years to complete. During this time, the US had got wind of a top-secret operation within the USSR. Many covert agents were dispatched to the region to investigate what was going on, however, none returned. Even those they had turned behind the iron curtain couldn't find out what was happening. After a while, the CIA put the idea of Hephaestus into the myth basket.

Myth, however, was very far from the truth. Once completed in 1977, Hephaestus was concealed in an undisclosed subterranean chamber beneath Volgograd, where it remained unchecked for many years. Those privy to its existence were enveloped by the knowledge and comfort of its presence.

Over time many discussions were had about its use. One of those was during the dismantling of the Berlin Wall. The hardline generals came close to making a decision but refrained, opting for the see-what-happens route. The next time was in 1991, when the USSR was formally dissolved.

At that time, Hephaestus had been woken and taken from its lair. It had been loaded onto a truck ready for transportation. A fresh intervention had Hephaestus sent back to hibernation.

Now, after the passage of so many years, Hephaestus was to be woken again. And this time, there would be no turning back.

The son of the gods was about to fulfill his destiny, and Europe would be torn asunder.

CHAPTER 1

JUST TWENTY-FOUR HOURS AFTER THE PHONE CALL FROM Mikhail Shatov, Knocker and I were on a plane to the historic city of Babruysk in Belarus. The final outcome of the whirlwind trip would prove most surprising, however, I get ahead of myself, so let's catch up first.

From my hospital bed the day before, while I was catching up with Knocker, I received a call from Mikhail Shatov. He proceeded to inform me about something called Hephaestus. "They are going to put it into action," he told me. "You have a week to track its location before final preparations are made to move it. To find out the rest, you will have to meet me in Babruysk, Belarus. I will contact you once you arrive. Millions of people depend on you."

The call disconnected, and I related the gist of the call to Knocker. My next move was to get out of the hospital in Ramstein and head to the local safehouse where I could reach out to Holly.

Her reaction was immediate. "Are you sure about this?"

"No, but it could be the break we need."

"What about this Hephaestus?" Holly asked.

"No idea."

"Do you mind if I break in here?" Sam *Slick* Swift asked, his red head popping into view on the video call.

"Please," Holly urged.

"Hephaestus, among other things, is the Greek god of fire and volcanoes. He is said to be the son of Zeus and Hera."

"You had me at fire and volcanoes," Knocker said. "Anything referencing that can't be good."

"It gets better," Slick said to us.

"Bollocks."

"Back during the height of the Cold War, a rumor surfaced regarding a top-secret project being worked on by the Russians, codenamed Hephaestus. The CIA attempted to infiltrate for intelligence but lost agent after agent. In the end, they conceded defeat, drawing the conclusion that it was a myth to draw in their people and kill them."

"Well, obviously, it isn't."

Holly said, "No, so it needs to be stopped. Go, meet with Shatov, and find out what he knows."

"I have a question," Knocker said. "What does Shatov gain by doing this? He's been the guy at the top all along. Now he wants to turn on the others. It doesn't make sense."

"Ask him when you arrive at the meeting," Holly said.

"I'll do that."

So, here we were, on a Cessna Citation flying into Belarus, hoping we wouldn't be locked up as soon as we set foot on the tarmac. The plane that was dropping us, was to leave right away. For this, we were on our own.

———

Meanwhile, in other parts of Europe, namely Finland, the skies over Helsinki were retaken by NATO forces and the Russian troops on the ground had dug in, ready for savage, street-to-street fighting.

NATO was gaining the upper hand, and it looked as though Russian troops were starting to pull back from the Polish border.

Or perhaps that was because of what they had planned next.

After touching down, we alighted and made our way to a vehicle that had been left for us. It was an armored Mercedes Benz E-class sedan with several hidden compartments.

Departing the airfield, we headed into the city, where a third-floor apartment had been made available to us. The thick layer of dust was testament to its lack of use. I opened the double doors onto the balcony, which overlooked the street below.

Knocker went to the refrigerator and looked inside. It was dark and empty, not even turned on. Next, he tried the cupboards and found the same. "Great, we're going to fucking starve and die from dehydration."

"Which one is it?" I asked with a grin.

"What?"

"Starve or dehydration?"

"Take your pick," he replied.

I looked at my watch. "Come on, let's go and find a café."

Knocker nodded. "Say, how are you feeling?"

"Like I could run a marathon."

"Truly?"

"What do you think? Of course not. Come on."

We locked the apartment, turning left once we hit the sidewalk, our search for refreshments taking us two blocks before encountering a small café. Ordering coffee, we also asked for fresh sandwiches to be made: ham and tomato for me while Knocker chose ham and cheese.

The coffee was good, strong enough to stand the proverbial horseshoe in. We sat for a while in silence, taking in our surroundings. It was Knocker who broke it. "Typical, isn't it?"

"What?" I asked him.

"It's like a bloody cliché in a fiction story that gets used time and time again. I mean, if I even read it, I'd say bloody hell, get something new, would you. But just fuck."

"Are you going to tell me?" I asked.

"I tell you, if anyone writes this story about us, the readers will roll their eyes and say, what a bloody pillock."

"Knocker—"

"Two guys sitting at a table over your left shoulder. Another at my right. Then there are two women in the corner just inside the door."

"Five of them?"

"Yes."

"You got a plan?"

His wry grin made me suddenly nervous. "Them

birds look a bit of all right. Might go and introduce myself."

"Knocker..."

He stood up.

"Sit down," I said to him.

"Don't worry, Reaper. If I get some action, I'll cut you in."

"That's what worries me."

Then came the wink, and I knew we were in the shit.

Turning in my seat, I leaned back against the wall, furtively dropping a hand to my Glock, and I waited.

Uninvited, Knocker joined the women at their table, and I could hear him speak. "Hi, ladies, nice evening."

They stared at him.

"Care to join us?"

Again, they stared at him, so he changed to Russian. "How's old mate Genady?"

Still, they stared at him.

With that, he stood up and returned to our table, nodding to the women. "Talkative lot."

"What did that prove?" I asked him.

Knocker shrugged. "I'm not sure yet. Let's see what happens when we leave."

Finishing our sandwiches, we put our coffee cups back in their saucers and rose simultaneously. Our movement elicited an obvious tension from our new friends.

Knocker and I walked outside and started along the sidewalk. Moments after our departure, we were being tailed, as expected.

The two women hung back, following at a distance

behind the trio of male operatives who took the lead. Five of them. Like that would be enough. Out of the corner of his mouth, Knocker said, "There is an alley up ahead. What do you think?"

"As good a place as any," I replied with a shrug.

Reaching the mouth of the alley, we stepped into the narrow opening on our right. I felt a rush of relief to see it was clear of any habitation, apart from an emaciated black and white cat. Heading deeper into the narrow thoroughfare, it wasn't long before footsteps could be heard behind us.

"Head or legs, Reaper?" Knocker asked.

Lately, we'd killed a lot of people without mercy. Maybe... "Fuck it, legs."

Turning suddenly, we took our escort by surprise, bringing up our Glocks and opening fire. Aim low, hit low.

The first two would-be killers went down screaming in agony as bullets tore through their legs, one receiving a devastating blow to his knee. At least he was still alive.

The third guy was seemingly more prepared than his comrades, his handgun already out.

Change of plan.

We shot him four times in the chest, fatally.

That left the female assassins who appeared frozen on the spot. Our Glocks were pointed at them but remained silent. Meanwhile, on the ground, the two wounded men squirmed and groaned in pain. Knocker moved forward and relieved them of their weapons.

"Okay," I said. "Listen up. Tell whoever it is that

sent you to leave us be. If not, we'll come knocking and kill every last one of you."

It was a hollow threat, but they didn't know that. Or maybe they did.

Keeping watch as we backed out of the alleyway, we returned to our apartment by a circuitous route, watching our back trail the whole way, then waited for a call. It had just gone seven that evening when it finally came.

"Mr. Kane?" It was Shatov.

I said, "We're here, what next?"

"Are you alone?"

"Define alone?"

"You and Mr. Jensen," he replied.

"Yes, but we seem to have found some others who want to crash the party," I informed him.

"I was afraid of that," he replied. "Our security is that good we don't even trust ourselves. There is a park. I will send you the coordinates. You will be there in one hour. Do not be late. This is your one chance, because after this, I will be dead."

The call disconnected and Knocker looked at me. "That was very dramatic."

"And possibly true."

"Yeah. This isn't going to end well, is it?"

"I guess we'll find out."

"Why would you say that his fears were true?" Holland asked.

"Because they kill their own, as you remember from what we've already told you over the previous days. Anyone who might prove a threat to their plans must be silenced. Shatov became that when he organized the meet with us."

"But why would he turn on his own after all that they put into place?"

"Because of what was about to happen," I replied.

Leaving the apartment once more, we drove to the park and climbed out of the Mercedes. It was already dark, but there was a good moon to light the way. We traversed a gravel path that wound through the park, one of many. The night was reasonably quiet apart from the traffic, which slowly faded the further we progressed.

Shatov was already there, waiting. He was seated on a bench holding a newspaper. I said, "I don't think the newspaper works."

He shrugged. "It's a comfort."

"What did you want to see us about?" I asked him.

"Hephaestus," he replied.

"What about it?"

"You have six days—make that five tomorrow—to stop it before it comes into play. Before it is moved."

"What is it?" Knocker asked.

"It is what you might call a myth," he replied.

"That doesn't help us any," I said impatiently.

"It is a super nuclear weapon capable of all but wiping out a small country," Shatov said.

I glanced at Knocker, who, in turn, gave me an incredulous look. I said, "Might be important."

"Yeah, but why is he giving it up?"

I turned to Shatov. "Why are you giving it up?"

"Because even though I love my country, would even go to war for it, I will not cause the death of millions this way. It is indiscriminate killing. Not war."

"Where is it?" I asked.

"Volgograd. Tractor factory."

WHAP!

The bullet came out of the darkness, punching into the general. He teetered for a moment then was helped on his way by a second bullet. "Shit, sniper," Knocker growled.

I grabbed Shatov and lowered him to the ground. Knocker grabbed his weapon and looked for a target. Beneath me, the Russian was all but breathing his last. I heard him say, "Stop…Grigori. You must stop…"

Then he was gone.

Another shot came close to Knocker, who suddenly realized what a stupid move he'd made by exposing himself. "Bollocks."

Dropping beside me, he said, "Time to go, boss."

"Truth."

Keeping low, we headed for a nearby garden bed filled with shrubs and bigger bushes. The shooter had to be equipped with night vision, that theory proved when more bullets chased us into the brush.

Crouching for a moment, we listened to our surroundings. Then we moved again, making a dash for our vehicle. Gunfire began to chase us through the park, but only briefly before it stopped.

Jumping into our Mercedes, we got the hell out of there. However, this was just the beginning of a running war with mercenaries, Russian soldiers, and assassins. If we thought Berlin had been bad, this was about to get a whole lot worse. And you could follow our passage by the bodies left in our wake.

CHAPTER 2

Arriving back at the apartment, I reached out to Holly, who got to work, organizing to meet us in Istanbul for a debrief. With our backup team established, we also knew that Volgograd would have to be done without them. It was good, however, to know their support would be available should the need arise.

But first, we had to get there. We didn't even manage to leave the apartment before our troubles commenced. Knocker called out to me: "We've got a black SUV in the street, which seems to be home to a couple of peeping Toms."

Crossing the room to the window, I moved the curtain aside so I could look out. Parked back from an orange streetlamp I noticed the vehicle to which Knocker referred. While I watched, a small, refrigerated truck pulled up below us. Moments later, the back opened, and a stream of armed shooters swarmed the street.

"Well, looks like the party is about to start."

Hurrying into the apartment's spare room, we picked up the AK-12s from the bed, donning the body armor and pocketing the spare ammo. Our chosen weapon, the AK, was a precaution in case they had to be abandoned on the go and were found by the Belarusian police. Blame the Russians instead of us. Even so, the ones hunting us knew who we were.

Slamming home fresh magazines, we worked the charging handles. Knocker looked across at me and said, "Back way, Reaper?"

I nodded. "Let's hope they're too focused on the front."

We went out onto the landing. The apartment building was hollow in the center, laid out around an internal staircase, each level having a landing that wound around at its heart. I peered over the edge, looking for our immediate threat. The landings were illuminated by dull orange sconces, but it was enough for me to see the figures urgently traversing the lower levels.

Unfortunately, it was also enough for them to see me. A shooter opened fire, forcing me back. Bullets whipped around us, screaming off the stucco walls.

Knocker said, "They've got night vision."

"Yes," I replied and leaned over to spray the figures with return fire. It was wild, but at least it would make them think twice.

Ducking back, I followed Knocker along the landing to the stairs and started down. "Bollocks."

Moments after the hissed curse, his suppressed AK opened fire. Cries of pain suggested he'd hit his target. Continuing his forward moment, he stepped over the two fallen shooters his fusillade had taken down. Reaching the second-floor landing, he stopped.

"We've got more coming up this way, Reaper," he called over his shoulder. "Take the landing."

I turned hard left and worked my way along the landing. Behind me, Knocker fired a burst then followed me. In battle, he reminded me of a centurion from a Roman legion. Hard-faced, calm, accepting of whatever fate was to come his way.

Ahead of me, the darkened shadows of the far end came to life. "Knocker, over the fucking side."

"Oh, for fuck's sake," he snarled as I planted my hand on the rail and hurled myself over the side, plummeting to the garden below.

Without hesitation, he followed me, landing with a loud thump in the middle of some evergreen plants.

"You okay?" I asked as I got to my feet and started to drag him erect.

"Every time we work together, we always seem to be jumping off things. It fucking hurts."

"Are you okay?"

"I'll live," he replied, following me toward the exit.

More lead hornets began to chase us out onto the street. I looked left and right. "Where did you park?"

"Further up the road so they wouldn't figure out where we were," Knocker replied.

"How is that working out?"

"Just shut up and run."

We galloped along like two old men weighed down by a ton and a half of bricks. Not because that's what we were, but because the hard landing following our jump had fucked us up.

"That's the last time I listen to you," Knocker said. "Next time, I just die. It'll hurt less."

Our track led us past the truck that had delivered the shooters. Even as we approached, I knew there was something there waiting for us. Two men leaped out and began firing. Our AKs came up and we returned their fire, sending them collapsing onto the asphalt.

What occurred next, we were totally unprepared for. The Mercedes sedan we'd been running toward blew up in a ball of orange flame.

The blast wave hit us flush, and it felt as though we'd run into an invisible wall. It sat us on our asses— literally.

"Shit, we're not getting out of here that way." I snorted. "Guess what? They damn well found it."

"Not my fault," Knocker replied, getting to his feet.

"Just shut up and keep moving."

Bullets commenced a scything swath through the air again as we slipped into a dark alley to our right. It was narrow and full of refuse and many discarded items. It was also fitted with a sensor light, which immediately detected our movement, illuminating the whole alleyway like daylight.

"Bollocks, Reaper, kill it," Knocker said urgently as he raced toward the alley mouth.

I brought up the AK and fired at the light. It shattered in a tinkle of glass, and darkness descended once more just as our pursuers appeared. Suddenly, I realized I'd just placed the ball squarely in their court. They had night vision. "You fucking dick."

The shooters opened fire, and we were forced behind a large industrial dumpster.

"What's wrong?"

"They've got NVGs, remember?"

"Never fear, Reaper old man, I have a Knocker plan."

"Good grief. Grenade?"

"No, something better." Suddenly the alley lit red, smoke rising seemingly from Knocker's fist.

"A flare? Where did you get that?"

"I brought it with me. Where the fuck do you think I got it from? Out of my ass?"

"That wouldn't surprise me," I said, firing along the alley.

"I needed one once when I was operating in Ethiopia—"

"Are you going to throw that fucking thing while you bore me with your story, or wait until it goes out?"

"Yes, right."

The flare arced through the air and landed in the center of the alley, separating us from the shooters with red smoke. Waiting a moment for it to distort their view, we began running for the other end.

Emerging onto a busy street, our head on swivels, we began searching out our best option. Then I watched as Knocker stepped into the middle of the street, stood in front of an approaching vehicle, and aimed his weapon at the driver.

The screech of tires told the story of what happened next.

"You shot the driver?" Holland asked, aghast.

Knocker rolled his eyes. "You truly are a bloody pillock, aren't you?"

"I beg your pardon?"

"*Sure, I walked out into the street and shot some poor sod who was just driving by.*" Knocker's voice dripped with sarcasm.

"*You didn't shoot him?*"

"*No, of course not. Bloody hell.*"

"*Then what did you do to him?*"

"*Stole his car.*"

"*Huh?*"

"*And got the shit shot out of it.*"

Knocker drove. The vehicle in question was a blue BMW M5 CS, which topped out at 190MPH. Knocker floored the gas pedal, and I felt as though my seat, with me strapped to it, was about to fly out through the back.

"Holy shit!" Knocker exclaimed as it shot forward. "This thing is a fucking jet."

"Yeah, well, take it easy. The last thing I need going through my mind is my fucking ass."

"Mate, not with my—whoa!"

He swung hard on the steering wheel, swerving to avoid the three SUVs coming from a side street on our left as we shot past it. "Bollocks, where did they come from?"

He put more pressure on the gas pedal, and I felt the BMW pick up speed. I glanced in the side mirror and saw them back some distance, but they were coming.

"You got them, Reaper?"

I rolled down the electric window. "Yeah, I got them."

Utilizing every one of his driving skills, Knocker trod hard on the brakes and took a hard right. I felt the BMW complain around me as the tires screeched and the vehicle shuddered violently with the sudden deceleration.

Then he floored it again, causing the rear end to whip around before gaining traction and hurtling forward with great speed. I looked out the back and saw the SUVs appear. This wasn't like the movies where it looks like the cars are going flat out. You could only go as fast as your surroundings allowed. To go beyond that can bring things undone, and fast.

A sudden drumming on the back of the BMW was an aural indication of the bullets being sent our way. The rear window blew in, spraying the interior, including us, with glass.

Knocker swerved. The rear of the BMW kicked around and then snapped back into line. A set of traffic lights ahead was fast approaching, as though we were the stationary object, and they were moving. One instant, they were green, and then they were amber, before turning red.

And we were doing eighty.

With no chance of stopping.

"Hold on to your bollocks, Reaper," Knocker said loudly. "This will make your butt pucker."

As those words left his mouth, we blew through the intersection, just missing two sedans and an SUV.

The first pursuer wasn't as lucky, smashing into a sedan. His SUV seemed to launch as if from a spring-board, twisting violently in the air before coming down onto its roof, sliding along the asphalt, and coming to a halt in the middle of the street. Definite points off for that dismount.

The two remaining SUVs went around it on either side.

"That got rid of one," I said to Knocker.

Knocker took another turn. "Shit, Reaper, all these idiots are going the wrong way."

I suddenly had hold of the invisible passenger steering wheel as we began swerving through the oncoming traffic.

More bullets peppered the BMW as the SUVs behind us started firing indiscriminately. "For a one-way street, it is mighty—"

Suddenly, an MH-6 Little Bird blasted low overhead. All around us, things began erupting as the rotary cannon on it fired rounds that ripped through the night. A vehicle in front of us exploded and flipped. It seemed to tumble straight at us and Knocker swerved violently. The burning vehicle ricocheted off the front left guard, scraping it but not doing too much damage. Two more blew, and then the helicopter pulled up and away.

"Get us off this street, Knocker," I snapped.

"I'm trying, Reaper."

"There, up ahead," I said, pointing at a cross street.

Knocker pulled across the two lanes of oncoming traffic and turned hard left just as the helicopter came back around and faced us head-on. I could see the asphalt leaping to life as the rotary cannon chewed a projectile trench up the center, heading directly for us.

"Ah, fuck." I closed my eyes and waited for the rounds to tear through my body. Then, just as the hail of devastation reached us, Knocker swung on the wheel...hard.

Two rounds punched through the trunk as we turned. It felt like the BMW had been kicked by a giant, but the machine kept going.

"That was close," Knocker said through gritted teeth.

"Just get us out of here."

We turned at the next intersection and found ourselves once more out on an open street. Then—

BOOM!

The helicopter was back and at its destructive best. This time, two rockets were fired from its pods. One blew the hell out of a storefront beside us, and the other hit a parked vehicle, sending it flying overhead.

"There," I said, pointing ahead and to the left.

"Where?"

"The tall building. It'll have a parking garage."

"I hope you're right because that prick is coming back."

It was now a race to see who reached their objective first. Us to the garage where we'd be safe from air attack or the helicopter where it would get another chance to wipe us off the face of the earth.

I glanced up and saw it coming, its navigation lights flashing in the night sky. We were cutting it a bit too fine. "Hurry up, Knocker."

"I'm moving."

"Move faster," I said.

His foot went down harder.

The helicopter was closer.

"Nope, won't do."

"You want me to fucking fly?" he snapped at me.

"It might help."

The helicopter fired.

Knocker turned.

A moment later and we would have died.

"That was close," Knocker said as we disappeared into the underground car park.

He engaged the brakes, and we came out of the BMW as it stopped. The two remaining SUVs entered the garage behind us, and we opened fire with our AKs. Bullets hammered into their vehicles and the front windshield on the nearest one shattered. I saw the driver and passenger jerk wildly under the impact of the rounds.

"Going left!" Knocker called out to me as he started to move.

"Going right!" I called back to him.

I took cover behind a parked Lada just as bullets peppered it and the windows disappeared. Leaning around the rear of the Lada, I fired back. A shooter took cover behind his SUV as my rounds hammered into the rear guard.

With that final burst, the AK magazine emptied, so I dropped it out. From the pouch on my chest I grabbed a fresh one and slapped it home, charged it, and was ready to get back in the fight.

Far over the other side, Knocker was putting his own stamp on the firefight. Through the rattle of gunfire, I heard him taunt, "Come on, you fucking pillocks, you can do better than that."

As I popped out to fire again, I caught sight of a shooter leaving cover as he tried to flank me. I aimed and fired the AK. The killer went limp and face-planted onto the concrete floor. The demise of their comrade elicited more gunfire, forcing me back into cover.

I waited before shooting again, picking the right time so I wouldn't get my head ventilated. I was about to fire again when another vehicle joined the others, and four more shooters tumbled from it. Shit.

"Knocker, time to go."

"Go fucking where?" he shouted back.

"Anywhere but here."

"Fine, you go first. If it's a good idea, I'll follow. If you get shot—if you get shot, I know it sucks."

"You're a brave man, Raymond."

"Fuck you. And don't call me Raymond."

After a couple of deep breaths, I broke cover and immediately sprinted toward the rear of the parking garage. I took up position behind a concrete pillar and waited for Knocker to join me.

Bullets chased him across the parking garage to where I was hiding. He ducked in behind me. I said, "I see you're still alive."

"Only just."

I fired at a shooter coming our way. I saw him fall and he dragged himself into cover. Behind me, Knocker looked around. "There, a stairwell."

"Fine. Go. I'll be right behind you."

Knocker left me in position and headed for the stairwell. Once he reached it, I followed. Tucked into the stairwell, I said, "Go up and get us onto the ground floor. We'll head out from there."

"Roger that." I reached for my cell, put the earpiece in for hands-free, and hit speed dial.

"Reaper, what's up?" Holly asked.

I fired at a shooter before turning toward the stairs. "We seem to have hit a snag."

"Is that gunfire I can hear?"

"A little bit."

"Shit, what's going on?"

"Shatov is dead," I told her as I climbed, determined to give her the basics of what I knew in case we didn't make it out of here alive. "His own people killed him. Hephaestus is a super nuke. It sounds like Grigori Igoshin has it and it is in Volgograd."

"Christ. Where?"

"The old tractor factory site. It must be in an underground bunker."

"So, what are you doing?"

"Right at this time, we're trying to stay alive. We need extract from the airfield. Can you do that?"

"Yes. I'll message you the details. Good luck."

By the time the call ended, I'd reached the ground floor. Knocker waved to me. "This way, Reaper."

I followed him through the foyer and out onto the front sidewalk. Knocker led the way, sticking to the shadows, using all we could for cover. In the airspace over the city, I could hear the helicopter waiting to strike at us. After a few minutes, Knocker found a vehicle, broke into it, and we were away in under a minute.

All we had to do now was get the hell out of Belarus.

CHAPTER 3

WHEN WE ARRIVED AT THE AIRFIELD, THE PLANE THAT Holly had organized was still ten minutes out. We were going to fly back to Istanbul, reset, and then make a run at the package.

Those ten minutes went by without a hitch, peaceful and quiet. Too peaceful. Too quiet.

After taking off, our track took us over Ukraine. We had no time to muck around, needing every available moment to do what was required. Yes, it was dangerous, and yes, it was a mistake. And we paid for it.

When the Cessna Citation was hit by the SAM, we were off course and over what was known as The Dead Zone. This was a disputed area that looked like no-man's-land from the Western Front. At its center was the old city of Pryluky.

Knocker and I were both sleeping after the night we'd had. The Cessna was cruising at 30,000 feet with the transponder pinging as a Ukrainian aircraft. What we didn't know at the time was that we were off course.

When the Cessna was hit, it threw the aircraft across the sky as though God had reached down and swatted it with a giant hand. My eyes came open instantly and I was suddenly aware of the hole in the fuselage, and we were losing altitude.

Knocker was looking at me, the howl of the wind around the aircraft almost deafening. "What the fuck happened?" he shouted.

"We're fucking going down," I shouted back.

"Do they have parachutes on this thing?"

"Front of the cabin."

I undid my seatbelt and climbed up, firmly gripping whatever handholds I could find. The Cessna was slowly flat spinning as it started to fall. I struggled against the centrifugal forces to the front of the cabin and found the cupboard where the parachutes were stored. Knocker was right behind me.

I grabbed one and passed it back with a pack that we'd need on the ground. "Here."

The second one went on my back. Then, with it secured, I opened the door to the cockpit and found one and a half pilots. The remaining one was of course dead. I turned back and said, "Time to go, Knocker."

He pushed up close behind me. I said to him, "Don't die on the way down."

"I don't plan to."

Then we cracked the door and left the stricken aircraft to finish its slow death.

"I'm sorry, I can't understand why you would take the flight that way with the risk that it carries. Since the Russians pulled out, that part of Ukraine is a hotbed of warlords and former Russian deserters trying to gain control of the region," German said.

"Not much left to fucking fight over," Knocker growled.

"That doesn't answer the question."

"Time sensitive," I replied. "We needed to get to Istanbul, reorganize and redeploy. Going the other way would have cut into our schedule."

"Instead, it cost the lives of two men and the British taxpayer millions of dollars' worth of aircraft."

"We all understand the risks we take when we sign up," I replied.

"It was a waste of life and blasted money!"

"And the opposite side of the coin was acceptable?"

He remained silent, so I continued with what happened next.

We landed in what was akin to a moonscape: myriad craters and destroyed vegetation. Detaching our parachutes, we started to look around. All the destruction was set against the backdrop of the ruin that was the city of Pryluky.

Knocker opened the pack and passed me a satellite phone. "Here, you call her."

"Why me?"

"Because you're the prick that got us into this mess."

"How do you figure that?" I asked Knocker.

"Because you were the one that told the pilots to go this way."

I sighed. "Fine, I'll do it. Just keep an eye out for anyone that doesn't belong."

I punched in a number from memory, and after two rings, Holly's voice answered. "Have you landed? You shouldn't be there yet. Which means there's a problem."

"You could say that," I replied.

"What is it?" she asked apprehensively.

"The plane crashed."

"You are shitting me. Tell me you are lying."

"No, it crashed all right. Knocker and I had to parachute clear. The pilots are gone, both dead."

"For fuck's sake. Where are you?" Holly asked.

"Ukraine," I replied. "Just outside of Pryluky."

"Shit, Reaper, that's in the middle of a fucking war zone."

I looked around at the devastation. "So it would seem."

"Reaper, we have visitors," Knocker said, interrupting.

I looked to where he was indicating, seeing four vehicles approaching along a cratered road. Two looked to be Humvees with 50-caliber machine gun installations on top of them. "I have to go, Holly. We're going to head into the city. I'll call you later for a pick-up."

"A pick-up? How the fuck do you expect me to extract you from the middle of a war zone?"

I could feel her tension coming through the phone. "I'm sure you'll think of something."

"Yeah, I'm sure I fucking will. In the meantime, I'll see if Slick can get a UAV in the air."

"It would be good if it was armed," I suggested helpfully.

"I'll see what I can do. Just don't get yourself killed before we get you out."

"Roger that."

The call disconnected and I turned to Knocker. I already had a Glock, but he reached into the backpack and passed me a few spare magazines of ammunition.

He said, "These aren't going to do much good in a fire-fight. But maybe we can get some weapons from those we kill if we need to."

I nodded. "Let's hope it doesn't come to that. In the meantime, let's get the hell out of here."

We started running across the landscape in the direction of the city. The approaching vehicles had to go the long way around while we could make our way across the rugged terrain. We reached the edge of the city well ahead of our pursuers.

"Wait," Knocker said. We stopped and he said, "You hear that?"

I listened for a moment and said, "It's the incoming vehicles."

"No, there's something else."

My eyes went to the sky, and it took a moment or two, and then I saw it: a small speck against the sky. "Aircraft."

As we watched we could see the parachutes open. Knocker said, "Bollocks."

"Who do you figure they are?"

"One guess."

"Grigori Igoshin."

"Or his people."

We'd find out later that it was a full company of specialists from Igoshin's mercenaries led by one of his many commanders. This one was Viktor Zobnin, former special forces who had fought across the globe representing Russian interests. Which meant, he and his team were assassins willing to take out anyone they came in contact with who didn't suit their agenda.

"Why is it that we've never heard of this Zobnin?" Holland asked.

"Because you haven't been in the right circles," Christine Ryan answered for me. "People like him operate in the shadows and only come out when things are getting bad."

"Which indicates how desperate they were getting to stop us from getting to Hephaestus," I told Holland.

"How many men did they send after you?" German asked.

"One hundred personnel."

"A lot of men."

"A lot at stake."

German nodded. "Continue."

Taking cover, we observed as the mercenaries came down. They landed on some open ground outside the city and quickly regrouped. While this was happening, the incoming vehicles changed direction toward the new arrivals.

What transpired next was confusing and had us scratching our heads. The approaching troops were obviously Russian. Of that, there was no doubt. However, the mercenaries waited for them to close within range before opening fire.

"Wasn't expecting that," Knocker said.

"Nope."

"Come on, let's get out of here."

I nodded. "Agreed."

We slipped back into the destruction that was Pryluky. During the height of the Ukrainian war, it had been the center of intense fighting between two divisions, going head to head in a battle that rivaled Stalingrad from World War Two. Over time, both sides pumped more personnel into the destruction until literally thousands were dead among the ruins.

Eventually, the Russians pulled out, as did the Ukrainians. What they left in their wake was a destroyed landscape, populated by deserters from either side, now split into factions and fighting their own wars among each other.

This was what we walked into.

I called Holly again. "We're in the city, but we're not alone. Igoshin has a company of mercenaries right behind us."

"Copy. Slick has a satellite over your position. He'll be able to conduct overwatch for a short time until we can get a UCAV overhead."

"Roger that."

"I'll put him on."

"Copy."

Slick came on. "Good morning, Excrement One. How are we this fine day?"

"Not funny, Slick," I growled.

"It suits because you two are always in the shit. And this time, you've exceeded your normal lofty standards."

"Remind me to shoot you in the face when we get back."

"I'll make a note. Now, let's see what we've got. You have a hundred-plus tangos coming into the city on your six. Not a good start."

"You should try being a pilot."

"True. Also, I'm picking up signatures of at least six unknowns closing in on your position from the west."

"Are they armed?"

"Wait one." A few heartbeats later and Slick said, "Yes, they are."

"Stupid question," I muttered. "All right, we're going to take out these guys coming toward us. We need their weapons and ammo."

"Roger that, Excrement One, I—"

"Call me that again and I'll excrement down your throat," I growled deeply.

"Copy, Reaper One. Time to get serious."

"Roger that."

We took up positions among the piles of debris at a choke point they would have to funnel through. While we waited, we were able to use our cells as comms devices. Once we were linked, the channel stayed open.

"Alpha, copy?"

"Copy, Reaper One."

"Good. We'll be on open comms for the duration or until our cells go flat. We still have full operational capacity on the sat phone."

"Roger that. Your friends are about five mikes out."

"What about the mercs?"

"They're coming too, but are a little farther out."

I looked at Knocker. "We need to get this done quickly."

Minutes later, our targets appeared. We came out from behind the rubble, our weapons pointed at them. "Drop your weapons!"

They stared at us in surprise but held onto their guns.

"I said, drop your weapons."

They all looked at each other. It was a sign that all wasn't well. Then they began speaking hurriedly. The second sign. I glanced at Knocker, and he knew what I did.

The move came from the sixth guy in line. He was dressed in rags and unshaven like they all were, but he was on edge from the start. His eyes seemed to dance with unease in their sockets. Then he moved.

He was holding what looked to be an AK-74M. He brought it up in a sweeping arc and was about to squeeze the trigger when Knocker put three rounds into his chest.

From there, it was a battle of the fastest. And the Glocks were easier to handle at speed than the AKs. Especially when those were pointed at the ground.

Firing my Glock twice, both rounds punched into the chest of the man I was aiming at. This wasn't the time for fancy shooting. Aim big, hit big. Before my target even started to fall, I'd switched targets and was shooting at the next guy.

Two falling when I shot the third. By the time that guy hit the ground, Knocker had the other two down. We hurried forward. One of my targets was still breathing, so I put a bullet in his head. Then I leaned down and picked up the best of the weapons before me. Knocker did the same. Then we took their ammo and checked them for anything else we could use.

Between them, they had two grenades and a knife. That was it. Better than nothing. Knocker checked the arms of one of the dead men and saw tattoos. "Russian deserters."

I nodded. "You ready?"

"Yeah."

"Let's go. Alpha, we're clear here and headed further into the city."

"Roger One. I have you on ISR. The mercs behind you must have heard the shots. They've fanned out and have quickened their pace."

"Copy."

We went further into the city and found an old building to hole up in for the time being. I looked at my watch to see that it wasn't even noon. "Alpha, copy?"

"Read you, Lima Charlie, One."

"We've gone to ground for the present. Keep an eye out, will you."

"I'm your eyes in the sky, One. I'm your all-seeing—"

"Shut up, Slick," Knocker growled. "You're driving me barmy."

"Roger that," he replied and went quiet.

"Well, Reaper, if there ever was a shit sandwich we could share between us, this is it," Knocker said to me.

"I agree. Except, I think it's gone beyond a sandwich. Maybe a big fat roast."

"Pass the fucking gravy."

We settled down to wait for what was coming next. It didn't take long. Slick came back to us and said, "Reaper One, your friends are closing in on your position."

"Copy, Alpha. We're moving."

"Just so you know, there was no deviation in their track."

I looked at Knocker, who nodded. "They can see us."

"Shit." I automatically looked at the sky. "They can see us, Slick."

"The only conclusion one can draw," he replied.

"Do you know how?"

"Has to be a drone."

"All right, we're going to find some cover."

"Might I suggest the high rise to your north?"

I looked north and saw it. At some stage, it had been maybe twenty floors high. However, it looked like it had lost at least the top five. The facade was filled with holes and all kinds of damage from the war. "Copy."

We started moving toward the building, climbing mounds of rubble where there was no way through. The building appeared to have been a hotel in its former life. The entrance had a large turnaround which was overgrown with bushes and trees. All the signage letters were gone from the façade, but we could still make out the writing, some of which was in English, that said it had once been a resort.

Entering the lobby through the entrance, once welcoming guests with a view through giant glass windows and doors, but now only the crunch of shattered glass beneath our boots gave indication of its former grandeur.

The interior was virtually destroyed. Tall columns now peppered with bullet scars, walls with holes, and all kinds of detritus littered the marble floor. In the center of the reception area was a small crater, a sign that a grenade had once exploded there.

We looked around. Knocker pointed at a wide staircase that led up to a mezzanine where there was a dining room. Or what used to be one. Tables were scattered everywhere, chairs overturned. The walls were full of holes, and like below, an explosion had shattered everything.

"We have to find somewhere to hide," Knocker said.

I looked at him and shrugged. "Up?"

"I don't know. If we go up, we need a way—"

"Who the fuck are you?"

We spun around, bringing our weapons up. Standing before us were five men. They had special forces stamped all over them, but they weren't. Not here. Which only left one scenario. "Private security?"

"That don't answer my fucking question."

The man was armed with a CQBR and wearing a full kit. Knocker said, "Consider me to be your fairy fucking godmother, you Welsh cunt."

Great start, intimidation.

I said, "We're here on holiday. What about you?"

"Nope, not good enough."

"Okay, can we at least do this later? We've got at least a hundred-plus tangos inbound."

"Fuck," the man growled. "I knew you pricks were trouble."

"Not our fault. We had to bail out of an aircraft that took a missile. Trust me, we'd rather not be here, but until we can get extracted, this is our lot in life."

"You got a name?"

"Kane. Father Grumpy there is Jensen."

"Fine. I'm Mako, he's Badger, Falcon, Smitty, and Dog."

I nodded.

"Follow us."

Mako led his team down the stairs and into another stairwell that took us below ground into the basement. The five flicked on flashlights, illuminating the darkness. "Just watch where you put your feet. There's all kinds of shit down here."

"Where are we going?" Knocker asked.

"You'll see."

Ahead of us, in the wall of a basement, a large tunnel opened up. Mako indicated it. "The city is riddled with them. It's like a rabbit warren."

For the next twenty minutes, we made our way beneath the city, finally coming out into an old public swimming pool complex. Mako turned to Badger and said, "Go and check our six. We'll be here for the next ten mikes or so."

"Roger that," the big, bearded man replied.

Mako turned to Knocker and me and said, "All right, let's swap pleasantries."

I nodded. "You know our names and that we were shot down. The guys chasing us, we think, are from Grigori Igoshin."

Mako let out a low whistle. "Friends in high places."

"That ain't the half of it," I replied and gave him the condensed version.

"Shit."

"What about you?"

"Mate, our problems pale compared to you. We were inserted here after a guy called Holliman, also known as Holyman."

"Who is he?" Knocker asked.

"Holliman is a former British SAS scouser who came here and never went home. It was thought his whole team was wiped out. Except after a while, word starts filtering out about some guy named Holyman drawing everyone together. The MOD wants us to find out if it is him."

"I wouldn't have thought he was much of a threat being here," I said.

"Former British soldier turned deserter heading up a massive cult that could become his own personal army."

"They're thinking ahead."

"Yes."

"How long have you been here?"

"Almost a week."

"No sign?"

"That's the strange part. We've been through this damn forsaken place and found nothing."

"Well, I hate to tell you this," I said to Mako. "We just fucked up your op."

The team commander was about to speak when he paused, listening to the transmission in his ear. When it was finished, he said, "Roger, Badger. Get back here."

"Trouble?" I asked.

"Your friends found the tunnel."

Leaving the swimming pool area we returned topside. From there, we made our way along a few streets before entering an old stone building. Mako took us straight down into the basement, where we found another tunnel.

This subterranean passage was only short, spanning about a block. It brought us up into a demolished housing unit.

Mako said, "We'll take another break here. Everybody, crack your rations, split them up." He looked at me. "I take it you guys don't have anything to eat?"

Knocker held up the backpack. "Sure we do. A bullet here, a magazine there."

"You're welcome to share what we have."

I nodded. "Thank you."

"Slick, you still online?"

"I'm here, One."

Mako frowned at me. I said, "I forgot to tell you we have our own support."

He shook his head. "Be fucked."

"Alpha, how far out is that UCAV support?"

"At least thirty mikes."

"Copy. Out."

Slick said, "You do realize I can still hear you, right. The cell is open."

"No shit."

"You have a UCAV on the way in?"

"Sure do."

"Shit. Bonus."

Slick broke into the conversation once more. "I'm not sure whether you want to know this, but there is a second force of unknowns headed your way from the east."

"How many?"

"Rough estimate, around four hundred."

"How far out?"

"Two mikes."

"Bollocks," Knocker growled. "How did you bloody miss them?"

"They must have been beneath the ground."

I looked at Mako. "We need to go. We've got four hundred inbound from the north."

Mako said into his comms, "Everyone, time to play hide and seek. Move out."

Our small band went back out onto the street and headed away from the two converging forces. Ahead of us, looming out of the rubble and ghostly landscape, was what looked like an old football stadium.

Mako said, "Let's head there."

I shrugged. "As good a place as any, I suppose."

Pressing forward, we entered the old stadium. Like the rest of the city we'd been through so far, it had borne the brunt of much devastation. It reminded me a lot of Pripyat. A city abandoned by its former occupants, a little worse for wear than when they'd left, complete with bullet holes and blast sites.

The main playing surface had evolved. The grass was long, and a shell crater split the halfway line. Somehow, a tree had found its way inside and looked as though it was flourishing. I looked around the arena and nodded toward the top tier on the far side. "Up there. It'll give us a good field of fire."

"It could see us pinned down as well," Mako said.

"We only have to hold for a while longer. Then our UCAV will be online."

"I hope you're right. If you're not, we're fucked."

CHAPTER 4

THE FIRST OF OUR PURSUERS ARRIVED ONLY MINUTES after we'd taken up our positions. They were locals or Tigers, as we had started to call them. Why? Because we needed to call them something and Tigers was it.

For some reason, Igoshin's people, led by Zobnin, had stopped. It was possible they didn't want to engage with the locals. I whispered into my hands-free, "How far out is that UCAV?"

"Few more minutes, Reaper."

"Speed it up." I lined up on a shooter who had just entered the former playing arena. "I've got him."

"Be my guest," Mako said. Then, into his comms, "Standby."

I stroked the trigger, and the AK slammed back into my shoulder. The 7.62mm round flew like a harpoon and smashed into the unlucky killer's head.

He dropped like a rock and disappeared into the grass. Moments later, all the others opened fire, and more Tigers fell under the withering fusillade. I looked for another target and found one creeping through the long grass toward the tree. It took two shots, but he died like his comrades.

Incoming rounds grew in intensity and were soon smashing seats all around us. I fired back at a shooter in the crater and saw him roll away from the impact.

Mako called over to me, "Kane, they're trying to flank us on the left."

I turned my head and saw a handful of people working their way along the third tier which was the same level as us. I opened fire and saw the impacts of the bullets in the seats. They shattered under the barrage of lead. It was then I became aware of something I hadn't thought about. The seats were plastic, and the bullets were tearing sharp pieces from them like daggers. I looked about me and saw the same with the seats in my current vicinity.

"Shit, fuck!"

"Reaper One, this is White Knight, over."

"Copy, White Knight," I said into my cell handsfree. "Good to hear your voice."

"Roger that. We're on station with a full payload of AGM-114 Hellfires. Just tell us where you want them."

8 Hellfires. What more could a man ask for? I looked over at Mako. "What is our location?"

He relayed me the coordinates and I passed them on. "I'm looking at an old football stadium. Confirm."

"That's it," I replied.

"Roger that."

"Knocker, are you still with me?"

"Copy, Reaper."

"Get higher and call them as you see them."

"Roger that, Reaper One. Bear with me, White

Knight, I'm just going to relocate. Be aware, this will be a danger close mission."

"Copy, danger close."

Finding another target, I opened fire and was about to shoot again when someone shouted, "RPG!"

The explosive projectile hit low and in front. The detonation ripped through the stadium, filling the air with scything shards. My cheek burned as a sharp piece of plastic sliced through the epidermis, leaving a razor-thin line that immediately filled with blood.

I dropped as low as I could, trying to protect myself. A storm of bullets followed the blast as the dark smoke rose into the air. I have no idea what they were shooting at because we couldn't see shit.

The urge was to change position, but if we couldn't see them, then we were reasonably safe. Right?

BOOM!

A second RPG.

"Motherfucker. Reaper Two, get a fucking missile down here."

"On the way, Reaper. Hang on to your bollocks. Send it, White Knight."

The missile screamed like an unseen freight train. On impact, it absolutely shattered the top tier where the flanking Tigers were beginning to gather. A giant crater appeared in the stand with no discernible base.

"Great, now get that fucking RPG!"

The first missile impact had the Tigers thinking twice about their next move because their rate of fire reduced substantially.

Moments later, a second missile hit in the region where the RPG had been fired from. If he wasn't killed, he'd be certainly reassessing his future.

I caught movement on the third tier to my right. Another group of shooters was trying to flank us. "Reaper Two, top tier on the right. Send it."

Knocker called it in, and a third missile crashed to earth, inflicting its own particular brand of devastation. I nodded with satisfaction. "Great work. Mako, are your people okay?"

"Affirmative."

"Alpha, tell me what you see."

"Looks like your friends are pulling out," Slick said.

"What about Zobnin?"

"Wait one."

I surveyed the scene before us as Slick attempted to locate the other threat. Then he said, "Reaper, he has vanished."

"A whole company?"

"Yes. They're not there anymore."

"Roger that."

"What is it?" Mako asked.

"Zobnin had disappeared." My mind ticked over. Then something clicked into place. "Did they have a metro in the city?"

Mako nodded. "Yes."

"That's how they do it. They're in the rail tunnels. Not just the others."

Mako said, "There is an underground station just outside the stadium."

"Then let's go and say hello."

Regrouping, we made our way down to the bottom level, then over to the stairs which led to the underground station built beneath the stadium itself.

Once we reached the platform area, we took up

positions once more. Then we waited for them to come.

Which wasn't long. We hadn't been in position long before the first scouts appeared. It was a sensible move. Send men ahead to recon the ground. Especially in unexplored territory.

Those scouts were not as vigilant as they should have been, and both died from knife slashes across their throats courtesy of Knocker and Badger. The bodies were dragged out of the way, and we waited again for the mercenaries to follow up.

They arrived in a line strung out like a herd of cows coming in to be milked. When they were finally closed in enough, we sprang the trap.

Gunfire, explosions, shouts, and cries of pain filled the underground station. I remember shooting one mercenary and then changing position to get a better line on another. In the first furious fusillade, at least ten mercenaries fell.

They retreated into the tunnel and Mako's men threw grenades after them. The roars of the explosions were deafening. A handful of shooters burst out of the darkness, trying to work around our flank, but died violently instead.

They tried again, this time with more men, for the same result. Then they pulled back and things went quiet.

"Slick, how far out is our extract?" I asked over the cell link.

"We can't get you out for another couple of hours at least, Reaper One."

I looked at my cell and noticed it was already screaming low battery. "All right. I'm powering the cell down. I'll reach out in another hour or if we need help. Keep that UCAV on station for as long as it takes."

"Roger that." I looked at Mako. "We need to keep moving, but first things first. Knocker, reequip."

"Roger that."

We moved through the bodies of our dead adversaries, selecting the best of a couple of AK-12s and spare magazines. We also stripped them of their body armor and shrugged into it. Now we were better off. I turned to Mako and said, "You've been here a while. Where to?"

"I know a place that might do."

"Lead the way."

Leaving the stadium, we worked our way four blocks through the city toward a large building. The damaged sign on it indicated that it had originally been a furniture manufacturing store.

Mako said, "We laid up here a few days back. It has a good lookout and a tunnel underneath that we can use if we need to get out in a hurry. And it also has a bonus."

"What's that?"

He nodded across the street. "An LZ."

I changed the direction of my gaze and saw the flat concrete area across the street. It looked as though it had once been a parking lot, but was now just a vacant piece of land covered in pavement.

Entering the building, we took in the derelict reception area at the front and, beyond that, the abandoned machinery and warehouse area. It was split over two levels. Dog went up onto the rooftop to keep an eye out while we rested.

———

"We've got movement," Dog said over his comms to Mako.

The team leader was immediately alert and came to his feet, saying, "Something's going down, Kane."

We grabbed our weapons and headed up to the roof, doing our best to keep out of sight. Hunched down beside Dog, Mako asked his man what was up.

"Three buildings down, across the street. There was movement in the doorway."

I stared at the point of focus and saw nothing.

At first.

Then, I detected a slight movement before making out a figure. I heard Dog say, "He's dicking us."

I looked around at the other buildings before going back across the rooftop to the other end. Crouched down, I ran my gaze along the street. I did it three times before I picked up the second dicker.

Moments later, Mako joined me. I said, "I've got another this side."

"You figure they're mercs?"

"No. I think they're the locals back for a second crack." I powered up my cell. As soon as I did, I was getting missed call messages. I called Slick.

"Where have you been?" he asked hurriedly. "You've got X-rays all around you."

"Yeah, we've just found the dickers. How many and where are they?"

"Everywhere," he replied. "Best number is upward of three hundred."

"Is that UCAV still on station?"

"It is."

"White Knight, copy?"

"Read you, Lima Charlie, Reaper One."

"Do you see what Alpha is seeing?"

"Affirmative."

"Drop a couple of Hellfires on them."

"Are you under immediate threat, Reaper One?" the operator asked.

"What does that have to do with it?" I asked him.

"I'm under orders to only fire ordinance if our assets on the ground are under immediate threat. Are you under immediate threat?"

I could see what he was doing. "Roger, White Knight, we are under immediate threat."

"Two rocket-fueled lances on the way, Reaper One."

I looked at Mako. "Get everyone up here."

Mako passed the order along. Moments later, I heard, "Reaper One, this is White Knight."

"Send traffic, White Knight."

"One, we have target acquisition."

"Send it, White Knight."

"On the way."

Thirty seconds later, the first Hellfire hit with devastating consequences. The building just behind the first dicker exploded violently. The sound wave and concussive blast smashed everything it touched. A ball of flame climbed into the air laced with debris.

"That's the first one," I said to Mako. "Second one shouldn't—"

WHOMP!

A second building further along the street from our position exploded the same way as the first. The noise of it rolled along the street and buffeted the building where we were.

"Threat neutralized, Reaper One," White Knight called over our cell net. "We'll remain on station. Holler if you need us."

"Copy, White Knight. Thanks for your assistance."

"No problem."

"Alpha, copy?"

"Copy, Reaper One."

"What do you see?"

"It looks like they are dispersing again," Slick replied. "They obviously didn't learn from the first time around."

For the next hour, nothing happened. The locals had broken up and melted back into the landscape. I was mindful that somewhere out there were Zobnin and his remaining mercenaries. We knew they would come, we just didn't know when.

I looked at my watch. Mako sat beside me. "How long?"

"Twenty minutes," I replied.

"What is next for you and your partner in crime?"

"An all-expenses paid trip to Volgograd."

"Just the two of you?" Mako asked, frowning.

I nodded. "We're a formidable team."

"Formidable or suicidal?"

"A bit of both."

"Reaper One, copy?"

I'd left the cell on but muted it on our end. "Copy, Alpha."

"Movement to your west. Looks like Zobnin is making another try."

"How many, Slick?"

"Best count is twenty."

"There's more out there somewhere. Find them," I said firmly.

We moved to the west side of the building and crouched down. It took a couple of beats to find what we were seeking, but we found it.

"They look like they're taking up covering positions for an assault," Mako said.

"The question is, where are the rest of them?"

"They know we have aircover," Mako pointed out.

I nodded slowly. "Slick, scan east of our position."

"Wait one."

A few moments later, he came back to us. "Ah, shit, you're right. They want you looking the—here they come."

"Get everyone to the east side, Mako."

Badger was already there. "We got trouble coming!"

"Shoot the fuckers," Mako called back.

"Don't have to tell me twice."

The air was suddenly alive with buzzing lead hornets as the mercenaries made their assault. A couple of smoke canisters were thrown to make things more difficult. Knocker was changing a magazine when he said, "I want to go back to Greece, Reaper."

"I'm with you there," I replied, firing at a ghostly figure in the smoke.

"Incoming!" The shout came from Smitty. "Mortar."

We all hugged the rooftop. The mortar round hit hard, opening a hole in the rooftop. The whole building trembled beneath us.

"Where did that come from?" I shouted.

"No fucking idea," Smitty called back. "I just heard it. Could be—here comes another."

This round hit toward the rear of the building. I heard Mako say, "Talk to me, Smitty. You're the bastard with the eyes."

Keeping my head down, I ran across to him. "You see it yet?"

"There, at our two o'clock. See the gap in the buildings? I'd say that's where it is."

"Right. Knocker, on me."

"Where are we going?"

"To see a man about a mortar."

"We're going to get shot at, aren't we?"

"You're getting shot at up here," I pointed out.

"You know what I mean."

"Yeah, I do."

We left the rooftop just as another mortar round sailed in. This one overshot, but it was still close enough to damage the building.

We had no idea what we were running into, and that was a cause for concern. Knocker said, "You want to go first?"

Hesitating momentarily before breaking cover, I started across the street and hit the other side at a run. Once I found cover, I waited for Knocker to cross. He joined me soon after, and we began making our way through the building opposite. It was the most direct route to the mortar.

The place we were in had once been a restaurant with apartments above it. We made our way through the dining area and then toward the kitchen. If it wasn't for the dust, grime, and rat droppings, we could have sworn the chef would be back to serve dinner tonight. What surprised us the most was a total lack of lookouts or others posted in the building itself.

After negotiating the kitchen, the rear door beckoned us. From beyond, we heard another mortar round take to the sky. I looked at Knocker. "You ready?"

"Yeah, let's do it."

I leaned on the door with a shoulder as I turned the latch, swinging it open with a rusty creak and bringing up the AK to firing level. Taken by surprise were the six people surrounding the mortar. I picked the first and fired before he could react. He dropped to the hard concrete beneath him, and I changed my aim to the next. Knocker had followed me through, and his weapon was already in action. His target was the loader for the mortar, hitting him in the head, then shooting the guy next to him more or less in the same place.

My second target died with three bullets in various parts of his body. Which left only two. Both seemed to be in shock at the sudden arrival of their executioners. They died beside their comrades.

While I swept the area, I asked Knocker, "You got something you can shit can that mortar with?"

He picked up a round and examined it. "I think so. I saw this once in a movie—"

"You fucking what? What did you see?"

"How they thump it on something hard and throw it like a grenade."

I shook my head. "Forget it."

"No, no, I can do this."

And he did.

"Fuck!" I blurted out and started running. Knocker

was right behind me, holding the mortar round. "Throw it the fuck away."

"Oh, yeah."

The round detonated and destroyed the mortar tube as we dove to the floor, taking shelter from the blast. I rolled over and looked at my friend. "What the hell was that?"

"Had to make sure I was far enough away before I threw it."

"Idiot."

"Reaper One, this is Viper One, over."

"Copy, Viper One."

"One, we're your ride home. Find us an LZ and we'll get you the hell out of there."

At last, the cavalry had arrived.

CHAPTER 5

Airlifted from Pryluky, Knocker and I were taken to Istanbul, and Mako and his team delivered elsewhere. Knocker and I met up with Holly and Slick at a five-star hotel. We were tired and worn down. We'd been on the go for weeks, and there appeared to be no end in sight for what we were doing. If anything, the game had been steadily intensifying.

We were all bunked in a large suite courtesy of the British government. Ordering room service, we enjoyed a great meal together, knowing we were relatively safe for the time being. But as we'd experienced throughout the mission, nowhere was totally safe.

Shatov was gone, but Morozov was the sole heir to the kingdom ruled by Lash. Beneath them was Grigori Igoshin and his minions, who seemed to be scattered across the globe like bloodhounds chasing an elusive scent.

Then there was Hecate, the deep-seated mole still in our midst. We had been successful in whittling down their numbers, but they still had dice to roll.

Hephaestus. The super nuke. There were only three days left on the countdown clock before it was moved. We had to locate it before then.

"We'll send you to Volgograd tomorrow," Holly said to us as we drank a beer. "I know it only leaves two days, but you need the rest. Ray proved that with his mortar stunt."

"It worked."

"It almost got us killed," I pointed out to him.

"What are we going to do after we stop this thing?" Knocker asked. "I know we threw a few things around, but we never really nailed it down."

"We kill Lash," I said, drawing everyone's attention.

"Miriam wants him alive," Knocker pointed out.

"I dare say I can remember that being said, too," German said, staring at me.

"He had to be stopped. It was the only way."

"The British government does not sanction the assassination of another country's leaders."

"It's a good thing that the British government wasn't there then."

"Are you saying that you actually assassinated the Russian president?"

"If you read a book, German, do you want to know the end before you get there?"

"What the fuck does that have to do with the question?"

"It's called being patient. We'll get there."

"Then I guess we'll have to work that out when we get there," I replied to Knocker. "Alive, we have to get him out of the country. Dead, he becomes someone else's problem."

"She'll bust your balls, Reaper," Knocker said to me.

"Then you'd better keep her tickling yours so she'll leave mine alone. Slick, where is that damn nuke?"

"I'm thinking it's under the old site," he replied. "I'm reasonably sure there is a bunker complex beneath it, built during the Cold War."

"How can you tell?"

He brought up a picture and circled what looked to be grates in the ground. "These look to be air vents."

"How do we get inside?" Knocker asked.

He grinned. "How is your Russian?"

Knocker glanced at me. "I have a feeling we're not going to like this."

I nodded. "Yeah."

"We're going to dress you up as a couple of old Russian generals."

"What do you mean by old? Actually, more to the point, why would a pair of old Russian generals be there?"

"Visiting the old battle site where you fought."

"Hang on, that would make us over a hundred," Knocker said.

"Around that," Holly said.

"Then how are we getting around if we're that old?"

"We'll be pushing you in wheelchairs."

"Now I've heard it all."

"Do you have a better idea?" Holly asked. "One that will get us in without raising suspicion. Without kicking something big off and without getting us all killed."

"Oh, we're all dead," Knocker said. "I just would have preferred it not to be on Russian soil."

There was a knock on the door, followed by, "Room service!"

My Glock came out immediately. I looked at Slick. "You?"

"What?"

"I know we didn't order anything else. Did you?"

His shoulders slumped. "Fine, I was hungry."

"Shit." I put my Glock away, as did the others.

Crossing to the door, Slick opened it and admitted a young woman who wheeled in a trolley containing three covered dishes.

Knocker stared and said. "You sure you're not starving?"

The young woman stopped in the middle of the room and began removing the lids. It was while she was doing this that I saw the small spider tattoo behind her right ear. Once again, my Glock was out, but this time, it was pressed against her ear. "Who the fuck are you?"

"I wondered how long it would take," she replied with a British accent.

"Knocker, the door."

He moved swiftly to take up position. I pressed the gun harder to her head. "Now, who are you?"

A click of fingers and Slick said, "You're good. Oh, you're good. But I know you."

"Hi, Slick."

"Who is she?" Holly asked.

The woman removed her wig revealing that she had blonde hair instead of black. "Kelly Morris, Strike Team Krait. Global."

I looked over at Knocker. "Open the door."

"You sure?"

"Do it."

When the door swung open this time, there were four others standing in the hallway. Only one of whom I knew. Knocker grinned when he saw her. "Hey, boss."

"You going to let me in or what?" Cara Billings asked.

"Sure. The more the merrier."

Entering the room, she wrapped her arms around my friend. "You look tired, Raymond."

"Don't call me bloody Raymond," he whispered in her ear.

Cara still looked the same, although her hair was longer than I was used to seeing it, and she had it in a ponytail. But other than that, the athletic build, the eyes, the face, it was all still there. She moved over to me. "Reaper."

I took her in my arms and hugged her. I said, "One day, we'll do this under different circumstances."

"I heard you were seeing an MP."

I grinned. "It's interesting. And not us."

"I understand."

Cara turned to Slick. "My best computer tech."

"Hey, boss."

Again, a warm hug and a kiss on the cheek. Then, "Hello, Holly."

"Cara."

"I came as fast as I could. Brought my best strike team."

"You did this?" I asked Holly.

"We're going to need help."

"Shit."

"So, this is the infamous Reaper I've heard so much about," a bearded man said, stepping forward. There was no tone, just respect in his voice. He held out his hand and I took it. "I'm Dick Hammond, team leader. This is Snake Lewis and Wombat Peters. Kelly you already met."

I nodded. "Wombat Peters? Australian?"

"Yeah, mate," Peters replied with a grin.

I looked at Hammond and gave him a wink. "Keep him away from Knocker. One lunatic is bad enough."

"You have one too, huh?"

"Shall we get down to business?" Cara asked.

"Let's."

Slick had been busy putting together an intel package. Pictures were laid out on the table. "Somewhere under this is a bunker complex. In that complex is something called Hephaestus."

"What is that?" Cara asked.

I looked across the table at her. "A super nuke."

"Good grief. What's it for?"

We gave her the short version. The one with Lash, Shatov, stuff like that.

I said, "We have two days starting tomorrow to stop it, or it gets out into the wild."

"But where to?" she asked.

"We figure anywhere from Germany to Great Britain."

"What do you need us to do?"

"Whatever you can," said Holly.

"Then I guess we need to tweak this plan."

"Let's take a break there," Christine Ryan said. *"I feel like I need a coffee."*

We had no complaints with that and after being told to be back in twenty minutes, we headed for the cafeteria.

"The mole has to know we're closing in on them," Holly said.

"I can't see any change in body language," I replied.

"You'll see it when we produce Lash," she said.

Knocker nodded. "At least we're almost there. I've had enough of this shit."

"Is Miriam going to be there?"

"Yes."

Holly's cell buzzed. She talked for a moment and then hung up. "Anesha Perera has just been named as Home Secretary. She's coming with Miriam."

"That's a big move," I said.

"She didn't mention it to you?" Holly asked.

"Not a word."

"Are you still planning on doing what Lash asked?"

"We made a deal."

"I still don't like it," Holly said.

"You don't have to, let's head back."

Returning to the conference room, we found a surprise waiting for us in the form of Anesha Perera and Miriam Craig. The new Home Secretary and the PM.

Miriam looked at Knocker then ignored him. I made eye contact with Anesha but left it there. It was German who spoke. "The PM and the Homeland Secretary have joined us for the final couple of hours for the debrief."

"Nothing better to do?" Knocker asked.

"I just wanted to be here when they took you away to an HMP."

"Still have the razor tongue."

It was all part of the façade. I said, "Shall we continue?"

"Yes, please," Anesha Perera said. "I'm looking forward to how you people saved the world."

Once we finished making the plan, we discussed it some more, tweaking any details that needed refining.

"So, you and Knocker dressed as old German—sorry—Russian generals are going to be wheeled in there to find a way into the bunker complex?"

"Yes."

"Okay, here is what I think you should do," said Cara. "We'll put Kelly in a nurse's uniform—"

"Like it already," Slick said. Heads turned. "I didn't say that out loud, did I?" His visage became almost as red as his hair.

Knocker slapped him on the back. "Welcome to my world."

"And Dick can be an orderly," Cara continued. "The others will be on site, and we'll be mobile in a van."

"Do you have a plane?" Holly asked.

"Don't worry, I can get us in there."

"Then let's get organized."

―――――

"Can't sleep," Knocker asked later that night when we were out on the hotel balcony together.

"No."

"Slick and that bird?"

"Yeah."

"I thought it was someone being murdered at first," Knocker said. "Then I realized what it was."

We heard a sound behind us and Cara appeared. "You too, huh?" I asked.

She nodded. "Is he murdering her in there?"

"Sounds like it," Knocker said. "I haven't heard anyone go like that since…"

"Since what?" Cara asked.

He glanced at me. "Never mind."

"I hope you weren't going to say me?"

"No, boss."

We looked out across the city. Istanbul was a mass of lights of different colors that seemed to wink at us. "How's Global going?" I asked her.

"It's going well."

"Thurston?"

"She's good. How's your sister?"

"Great. She's doing some online degree. Easy to see where the brains went."

"Shit," said Knocker. "While we're sharing, my ex-wife is the new British PM."

"Gone up in the world," Cara said.

"Still likes to kick a guy in the bollocks," he replied. "But I always knew she was going places. Just not with me."

"I really can't imagine you tied down, Ray," Cara said.

He gave her a big shit-eating grin.

Cara held up her hand. "Forget I said that. I'm sure you've been tied down more than once."

There was movement inside. We all turned to look and saw Slick at the minibar in his underwear. We walked inside. He turned and saw us. "What's going on? Can't sleep."

I shook my head. "Something like that."

He shrugged. "Me neither, must be the mission."

"Sounds like it's a mission," Knocker said with a grin.

"What?"

Suddenly, Kelly appeared. Just in her panties. They were black and fitted her like cutoff shorts. "Did you find any ice, Sammy?"

He indicated at us. She turned and smiled. "Hi. Can't sleep?"

"No," Cara replied.

"Me neither. Must be the mission." Then they disappeared back into their room.

Cara rolled her eyes. "Anyone for a beer?"

We arrived at the airfield the following morning to be greeted by one of Global's new stealth transport aircraft. It was a converted Airbus A400M Atlas. Don't ask me how it worked, but it did.

All of our required equipment and weapons were loaded. Our special effects people came with us. While they worked on transforming us on the way over, I felt like I was about to star in a Mission Impossible movie. When they were done, our metamorphosis was brilliant.

While we were being made over, the others kitted out the van we were to use. Comms kit, cameras, everything that could be thought of. Global was like MI6's bastard brother as far as equipment was concerned. And I say that in a good way.

Cara came over and sat beside me while the makeup artist worked on me. "How goes it, Comrade Colonel?"

"I can't believe how quiet this plane is," I replied. "Especially for a prop aircraft."

"Our techs are pretty good."

"They are."

"Listen, we're not going to have much time on the ground to get everything unloaded, so we'll need to be quick about it. It's been timed that we'll touch down late afternoon so you can get to the site while there is still daylight but less people."

I grinned. "Don't look at me, I'm an old man."

"Very funny."

"Has Slick found a way in?"

Cara nodded. "Better than that, Boy Wonder has found floor plans for the whole shebang."

"All he has to do is narrow down where it is."

"And he's done that too. There are three bunkers attached to the complex that possibly may contain it. They appear to have elevators to the surface. You'll use one of those to get in. It looks like everything is interlinked."

"I knew Ferrero picked him for a reason when he put the team together."

The plane shuddered as it hit some turbulence. Cara said, "Just don't hang around after you get the C4 on it."

"Wasn't planning on it," I replied.

"Once you're out, we'll meet the plane at the extract point."

"You never said exactly where that was."

"Outside Volgograd, there is a long stretch of double-lane highway we can use."

"How long," I asked.

"Long enough for the plane to land," she replied evasively.

"Cara."

"Three-thousand feet."

"What is the tactical takeoff distance?"

"Thirty-two hundred."

So we would be two hundred feet short. "Shit."

Cara smiled. "The captain assures me the numbers are only a guideline."

"I hope so, or we'll be the next innovation of a Russian plow."

"Trust me."

"Hey, Knocker," I called over to him as his artist was finishing off.

"What's up, Reaper?"

"We're short on the extract takeoff."

"How far?" he asked, seemingly unconcerned.

"About two hundred feet."

"Don't worry about it. The numbers are only a guideline anyway."

Cara's grin grew wider. "See."

"Great, just as my ass goes through my brain, I'll be thinking that the numbers are only a guideline."

She slapped my shoulder. "That's the spirit."

The Atlas shuddered again, and I wondered how long before the makeup artist stabbed me in the eye with something sharp. She kept working until I was done. I looked into the mirror before me and decided that it would be a shame to destroy all her hard work when it was time.

"Ah, Comrade, you look so fucking old," Knocker said to me in Russian.

"Speak for yourself, you old roadmap."

We changed into old uniforms and prepared ourselves. The wheelchairs were specially made with compartments underneath with hidden MP5SDs and ammunition. The blankets that would be draped over us would hide it all, including the Glocks we would be using. Even the van had been modified to accommodate our ruse. Normally on an op like this, we would go in using local weapons and hardware. Not this time. We didn't care if they knew who was responsible.

I walked over to Slick, who was deep in thought as he worked on fine-tuning last-minute details. I placed a hand on his shoulder, causing him to look up. He jumped. "Be fucked, Reaper—wait, is that you, Knocker?"

"No, it's me," I replied.

"Man, those people do good work."

"That they do. What are you up to?"

"Just last-minute things with your IDs and stuff like that."

"Anything about the target?"

Slick punched a few keys and said, "This is the target, as you know. I'm reading heat signatures at different points throughout."

"Looks like a fucking trap," I replied.

"My thoughts exactly. Can we afford to go in?"

"Can we afford not to?" I asked him.

"Stealth will be the key," he pointed out.

"Especially with no air support." I patted him on the shoulder. "Just do what you can, Comrade."

"Did I hear someone say no air support?" Cara asked.

I looked at her. "Is there something you're not telling me?"

"You're working with Global now, Reaper. We'll have a Dragon on site ready to go."

"A Dragon?"

"It's a converted C-17 weapons platform with stealth capabilities. Think Specter Gunship, but with bigger balls. My present to you, Baby."

"Callsign?"

"Leopard One."

"Wait, why didn't I know about this?" Miriam Craig asked, interrupting.

"Welcome to our world, Prime Minister," German replied.

"First, you weren't in office," Knocker replied. *"And second, it's best to ask forgiveness than permission more often than not."*

"But you had a military asset over a foreign country," Miriam pointed out.

Holly said, *"Ma'am, the aircraft was a private contract platform, and at the time, NATO was still engaged in a war with the Russians."*

"Not much of one."

"Yes, but some of their forces were still engaged, even if only minimally."

"I see."

"Was it necessary?" the Home Secretary asked.

"It possibly saved their lives, ma'am."

"Then let's hear it."

"Yes, ma'am."

CHAPTER 6

THE ATLAS TOUCHED DOWN SMOOTHLY, AND WHILE IT was taxiing, the ramp came down and the van exited with us onboard. There was nothing wrong with the length of runway for the insertion, but it wasn't to be used again, just in case.

From the airfield, we drove into Volgograd and to the target. The only last-minute change we made was to leave Slick on the Atlas, where he was better equipped to do his thing.

"Coming up on target."

The sun was almost on the western horizon when we arrived. We were let out of the van and headed toward the site. Kelly was wheeling me, and Hammond took Knocker. They wheeled us toward the insertion point, and we were almost there when a soldier appeared.

"Halt."

"What is wrong?" Kelly asked in flawless Russian.

"What are you doing here?"

She indicated to Knocker and me. "Last requests."

He frowned. "What?"

"Do you not see the uniforms?"

"I do not recognize them."

"No."

"They were with the Thirty-seventh Guards Rifle Division. Many of them died on this very ground, idiot," Kelly snapped.

"Really?" He stepped closer to us. "Did you fight here, old man?"

Knocker coughed and spat on the ground. "Fucking toy soldier. We've seen more dead than you've had fucking prostitutes. The only way an impostor like you could get a woman."

"What?" the soldier asked incredulously.

"We fought shoulder to shoulder with our women, Comrade asshole. By day we killed Nazis, by night we fucked. Then the next day, we did it all over again."

"Listen to me—"

"Stand to attention!" I snarled at him. "Don't you realize a general officer when you see one?"

The soldier stiffened.

"We may be old, but we still command your respect," I snapped.

"Yes, Comrade General."

I coughed then said, "Now, fuck off while we say goodbye to our fallen comrades."

"Yes, General."

The soldier hurried away. In my ear, Cara said, "Wow, guys, that was impressive."

"Knocker?" I spoke.

In his best old-guy voice, he said, "I think I shit myself."

I grinned. "Alpha, we are Charlie Mike."

"Roger that."

"Reaper One, your insert should be just ahead of you."

"Copy."

It looked to be a partially concealed shed with a sign on it saying *KEEP OUT*. And to those who didn't know, that's what it was. But on the other side was an elevator, which would take us thirty feet down. "Slick, what are you seeing?" I whispered.

"I count maybe twenty shooters under your wheels. There could be more."

"Any outgoing comms traffic?"

"Bits and pieces. I expect it to pick up once you're in there," he replied.

"Can you kill it without killing ours?"

"Should be able to."

"Then do it."

We reached the doors and opened them. On the other side, as predicted, was the elevator. We entered and in the top left corner was a camera. We disabled it and then prepared for what was to come.

Knocker and I came out of our chairs and peeled off our faces. While we did this, Hammond and Kelly extracted all our equipment. We prepped our weapons and grabbed flashbangs. I turned to Knocker and held out a hand. "Give it."

"What?"

"You know what."

He reached into his pocket and passed over a frag-mentation grenade. "You're no fun."

"This is not the place for that."

"But it is for C4?"

"Are you two like this all the time?" Hammond asked.

"All the time," I replied.

"You're like an old married couple," Kelly said.

"You should see us when the chips are down and the shooting starts."

The elevator bottomed out, the doors slid open, and we went to work.

There were two shooters on the other side of the elevator door. Knocker and I dispatched them with well-placed shots and they fell without making a noise. Coming clear of the elevator, we found no more immediate threats. In my ear, Slick said, "Take the left hallway. The first checkpoint should be down there."

"Roger that. We're moving."

Continuing along the hallway, we stopped when we reached the door. Once we were ready to breach, Knocker opened the steel door. Hammond was the first guy through. Kelly followed him and they both swept the room, but it was empty. I said over the comms, "Slick, we've got a dry hole, direct us to the next one."

"Roger that. Turn to your right outside the door."

Once more, Knocker led the way, and he was about to walk back out through the door when Slick called back over the comms, "Hold position. You've got an X-ray coming your way."

Knocker held just inside the door, his finger on the trigger. I could see him counting inside his head, and when he got to three, he stepped out into the open, the MP5SD up to his shoulder, and he stroked the trigger.

Bullet casings rattled on the floor. The rounds, which exploded from the end of the suppressor on the submachine gun, smashed into the chest of the sentry. He gave a yelp of pain before falling to the floor in an untidy heap. Then I heard Knocker say, "We are clear."

Slick said, "Continue along the hallway. A little farther down, turn left. From there, you go straight for a bit before turning right."

Following his directions, when we turned right, we found ourselves at the entry to a large room. It looked as though it had once been a laboratory. On the far side of the room was a door, but we hadn't moved far into the space when a shouted warning came from Slick, and six men broke through the door.

"Lookout!"

Slick's outburst was not normal radio protocol, but I guess that was all he could do upon seeing the shooters suddenly manifest. The four of us dived behind old desks and benches as bullets sliced through the air, destroying everything they touched.

Glass, metal, and wood splintered, falling on us like rain from above. All kinds of detritus seemed to land all over my body. I could hear the shooters calling out to each other, urging themselves to push on.

Kelly cried out, "On the left."

I rose and saw two shooters trying to flank on that side. We opened fire at the same time and both men fell flat to the floor, blood draining onto the cold concrete.

To our front, Knocker and Hammond were working on the others, one of whom fell back after being clipped. Wounded or dead, I had no idea. But three remained.

With the magazine I was using empty, I quickly reloaded. I then sought out my next target. But I was forced back behind the desk I was using for cover. Bullets hammered at it, chewing it to pieces.

"I'm pinned," I called out.

"On it," Kelly said. "Flash out."

I tried to hunker down even further. The flashbang went off and the sound echoed throughout the old lab. Even as the sound dissipated, we were up and moving forward.

All four MP5s rattled off rounds and the remaining shooters went down, the room finally secure.

"Slick, we're secure, moving on."

"Roger."

Beyond the door that the Russians had come through was another hallway. "Slick, what's at the other end?"

"Something big," he replied.

"What do you mean?"

"The area is big. Like a huge workshop big."

"Targets?"

"None at this point in time. There are some coming around on your six."

"Roger that."

Opening the door, seeing what lay beyond was not an everyday occurrence. It was an old underground rail yard. We stood on a landing, surveying the enormity of such an engineering feat. The stairs went down at least two levels, if there were levels to be had. Instead, it was like a giant concrete cavern.

At its heart was an old diesel engine pulled alongside a scaffold. There was also a crane and two flatbeds hooked to another enclosed freight car. Then there was the other equipment and stacks of crates. Like I said, an underground railyard.

"Reaper, be advised, you now have two groups closing on your position," Slick said.

"I was right, it's a trap."

"What about the nuke?" Knocker asked.

"Without a doubt, it's not here," I replied. "Holly?"

"Copy?"

"I'm calling it. The nuke isn't here. If something happens, get out and don't worry about us."

"Roger. We'll send Wombat and Snake to you."

"Copy."

"Good luck."

"Okay, let's find somewhere to fight."

Knocker started down the stairs. "I always wanted to be a train driver."

"I'm more of a crane driver myself," Kelly said, following him.

"Hammond?"

"I'll take the flatcar."

"Roger that. I'll set up in those crates," I said, indicating off to the left.

I followed them down the stairs and I made my way to the stacks of wooden crates. They were bigger than they appeared from above. On the side was some faded writing. I couldn't quite make it out. "Comms check."

They all called in.

I reached out to Slick. "Talk to me, buddy."

"You've still got a good number of tangos coming your way. They should be on top of you in two mikes."

"Roger that. Any activity outside the box?"

"Negative."

My shoulder leaned against a box. It was heavy

and took my weight. After a brief moment, I heard Knocker in my ear. "How long you figure this thing has been here, Reaper?"

"About fifty years," I replied.

"What makes you think that?" he asked me.

"Have a look at the tunnel," Kelly said.

After a couple of heartbeats, I heard, "Oh, yeah."

Up above the tunnel was a number. The year it was constructed. "What do you figure they used it for?" I asked.

"Besides storing a world killer?" Hammond asked.

"Yeah."

"I would say that they stored ballistic missiles down here," Knocker replied.

"Okay, genius," I said. "I'm listening. Tell me."

"See that flatbed?"

"Yeah."

"See the racks on it? Designed to carry missiles."

"You sure?" I asked.

"How the fuck should I know?" he shot back at me. "Seemed like a good thing to say."

I heard Hammond chuckle. "You two are bizarre."

I said, "It helps deal with what's about to happen."

"Heads up, Team," Slick said. "Things are about to get gnarly."

"Fucking gnarly?" Knocker muttered. "Are you a skeg-head or something?"

"A what?" Slick asked.

"A surfer, dude, a bloody surfer."

"Knock it off, here we go," I whispered as the door at the top of the landing opened.

"Movement on the other," Kelly whispered.

"This is Krait Three, we're five mikes out."

"Copy," I whispered.

As I watched, the Russians began to filter down the stairs. We waited in silence as they made their way to the bottom, fanning out immediately to begin their search for us. I held my breath for a moment and then said, "Now."

Chaos broke out all around. My MP5 opened up, bullets exploding forth. My target cried out and fell to the floor. Behind him to the right, another Russian tried to dive for cover, but one of the others clipped him.

A Russian took cover behind one of the flat cars and was firing close range at Knocker on the engine. Knocker ducked down as bullets from the Russian weapon ricocheted all around him. Over the open channel, I heard, "Of all the—motherfucker, bollocks."

"You, okay, Raymond?"

"Don't fucking call me Raymond. Fucking pillock."

He was fine.

From where she was, Kelly had a better line of sight on the shooter than either Knocker or me. She let loose a burst and the would-be killer died.

"You're welcome, Raymond," she said sarcastically.

"Bitch."

"Love you too."

"You hear that, Slick? She's not your woman anymore."

"You'd better have a big trouser snake, Knocker, because compared to my man, I think you'd be lacking."

"Christ," Slick growled. "Don't tell everyone."

"Big and proud, Baby. Big and proud."

"You hear that, Reaper?" Knocker asked. "The red-headed wonder is hung like a horse."

"Christ, I command children," I growled.

I opened fire at another shooter, who stumbled and fell. He crawled behind a stack of crates, and I saw an opportunity. "I'm going out, don't shoot me."

"What the fuck are you doing, Kane?" Hammond asked.

"Getting a prisoner."

"Can't it wait?"

"No."

I slung the MP5 and took out my Glock before breaking cover. Firing in the rough direction of a nearby shooter as I ran, I ducked down behind an old motor on wheels just as bullets started to ping off it. As I went to move again, another burst of fire stopped me. "Son of a bitch."

I fired three times in the general direction. That just drew more incoming rounds. I repeated the dose and then ran. When I reached the wounded Russian, he was seated with his back against the crate. Blood was starting to pool around him. His face was gray.

"Not doing too good there, Comrade," I said as I crouched beside him.

"Fuck you," he moaned.

"I'm guessing without help, you're pretty screwed."

He grunted.

"Where is it?" I asked him.

"Where's what?"

The gunfight continued all around us, but we were out of sight. "The nuclear weapon?"

He gave a weak smile. "Gone."

"Gone where?"

"I don't know. They said something about a train."

"Where was the train going?"

"I don't know."

He was of no further use, so I shot him.

I stared across the table at the two women who had joined us late. Both seemed unperturbed by what I'd just told them. A couple of moments later it was Miriam who spoke. "Why?"

"Because he was dying, and while he breathed, he was still able to communicate with his comrades."

"So, you murdered him."

"If you say so. I'd prefer to say that I eliminated a threat to our mission."

"Your mission was worth becoming a murderer?"

"His life against millions. You work it out." I glanced at Anesha. She remained unmoved, but I could tell she understood.

Miriam nodded. "Okay, I just wanted to understand."

Now that he was dead, I said into my comms, "It's not here. Time to get out."

"Anytime you're ready," Hammond said.

"Wombat, Snake, where are you?"

"Look up."

I found them on the landing we'd used to come in. They were acting as snipers and doing it well. I said, "Everyone out."

Pulling back, we began to climb the stairs, reaching the landing then making our way back to the elevators and up to the surface.

"Reaper, copy?"

"Roger, Slick."

"You may have a problem."

The doors to the elevator slid open and we pushed open the shed door to step outside. It was about then that we saw the problem.

"Ah, fuck," Knocker growled.

"This is interesting," I muttered.

"Drop your weapons on the ground!"

My eyes ran along the line of Russian mercenaries in front of us. "Thirty, you think?"

"Closer to fifty," Hammond said.

"A lot either way."

"Yeah."

"Drop your weapons!" their commander ordered again.

"Leopard One, copy?"

"Copy, Reaper One."

"I need you to do me a favor. Can you see this?"

"What are you doing?" Hammond asked.

"Leopard, I need danger close fire support. Put it on top of these assholes."

"Roger. One-oh-five?"

"That'll do."

"John Kane, order your people to put their weapons down," the commander said.

"Are you Viktor?" I asked. "You're not Grigori, so you must be Viktor Zobnin."

"Very good, now do as I say, or I will start shooting you. The woman first."

"Ready, Reaper One?" asked the controller on the C-17.

"I want the first one fifty to their rear before you drop it on them, copy?"

"Copy."

"Send it."

CHAPTER 7

THE FIRST 105MM ROUND DROPPED WHERE I WANTED IT to. Fifty meters behind the line of mercenaries. It shook them to their cores, and they turned to see what the hell was happening. We chose that moment to throw ourselves backward into the elevator. The doors closed, and hell rained down from our own God of War.

The ground beneath us shook violently as the shells hammered into the earth outside like lightning bolts in a storm. We crouched low with our hands over our heads just in case a round strayed off course. Not that it would have mattered. If it did, we were fucked.

"Check fire! Check fire!" The command rang out over our comms.

We slowly climbed to our feet, and I pushed the doors open. What greeted us wasn't a pretty sight. Craters and body parts were scattered everywhere. The mercenaries were mostly all dead. Those that weren't wished they were. I found Zobnin lying among the detritus of his people.

Suddenly, the van raced into view, Holly behind the wheel. "Come on."

We ran toward the vehicle and piled into it, slamming the door behind us. Holly floored the gas pedal, and the van shot forward.

"That was interesting," Knocker said, breaking the silence.

"Very," I replied.

"You brought fucking fire down on top of us," Hammond snapped.

"Better than them doing it. Not the first time."

"You're fucking crazy."

"You should see me when I'm pissed."

"It's not bloody funny."

"Dick, leave it," Cara ordered.

"Ma'am."

While he simmered, I said into my comms, "Talk to me, oh wise one."

"Reaper, there are response teams closing in on your position from all sides. They've got blanket coverage of the city, and they mean to use it."

Leaning forward, I looked out through the front window of the van. The sun was down, but the van was too big of a target to make it back to the extract with the whole of Russia closing in on it. Then I saw something we could use. My finger stabbed at it. "There, that truck, stop in front of it."

"What are you doing, Reaper?" Knocker asked.

"Getting us a buffer. Can you drive it?"

"Bollocks, I thought you'd never ask."

The truck was a Scania with a tri-axle trailer on the back. It's amazing how much motivation the pointy end of an MP5 provides a person on the receiving side. We apologized for stealing his truck of course, but took it anyway.

Knocker drove, I rode shotgun, Kelly and Wombat riding in the sleeper. We were pulling a trailer, but it wasn't too heavy. I said over the comms, "We'll lead. You follow."

"Roger."

I turned to Knocker. "Let's do this."

He engaged the truck's gear lever and it pulled away. The van settled in behind us and we started toward the secondary airfield. The deep-throated growl of the prime mover sounded like a metal beast as we took our first corner. It was fully dark and things were about to escalate out of control. It was then I heard Slick say, "Reaper, prepare for imminent contact."

The roar of engines echoed through the narrow streets as the truck and van barreled forward, their tires screeching against the asphalt. Behind us came a convoy of black SUVs, bristling with armed shooters, set on stopping us from reaching our destination. Both vehicles, by now, had multiple holes from rounds in them, and so far, we'd been lucky. In saying that, we now had another problem. Above, the rhythmic thump of helicopter blades cut through the night, its mounted guns trained on us.

Knocker swerved the truck sharply to avoid a parked car, its massive frame barely fitting through the tight alleyway.

"Where the fuck are you going?" I snapped.

"Shortcut."

"Shit."

The van followed closely, Holly expertly navigating the twists and turns. Bullets ricocheted off the pavement and buildings, sending sparks flying and shattering windows. The SUVs maintained their pursuit, their occupants leaning out of windows, firing indiscriminately.

The Scania came hammering out of the narrow street. "Hang on," Knocker called out.

The beast leaned hard to the right and I was forced to grab at the door handle to stay in my seat. I glanced into the side mirror to see if the trailer was following us around. It leaped wildly and came up before crashing back down.

The helicopter swooped lower, its spotlight illuminating the chaotic chase below. The door gunner opened fire, rounds peppering the ground around the truck and van. Holly jerked the wheel, narrowly avoiding a direct hit. The Scania took the brunt of the assault, its sides absorbing the impact.

As we approached a busy intersection, Knocker blasted the horn, scattering pedestrians and vehicles. The van darted through the gaps, its smaller size allowing it to weave through the traffic. The SUVs, undeterred, followed suit, their drivers showing no regard for the chaos they were leaving in their wake.

The helicopter, now hovering directly above, unleashed another volley of gunfire. Knocker, spotting an upcoming overpass, made a split-second decision. The truck veered sharply, heading straight for the underpass.

I closed my eyes. "Ah, shit. It won't fit."

"Yeah, it will."

"No."

"I guess we'll find out."

It did. Just.

The van followed us, the SUVs close behind. The helicopter, unable to follow directly, circled around above.

Under the cover of the overpass, the truck and van momentarily disappeared. The SUVs, now bunched together, struggled to maintain their formation. Emerging on the other side, the Scania accelerated as Knocker floored the gas pedal, its engine roaring with effort. The van, keeping pace, swerved to avoid another hail of bullets from the pursuing SUVs.

Streetlamps became a blur as the chase continued. The armed shooters in the SUVs and the relentless helicopter above remained hot on our trail.

"We need to shake them somehow," I called over to Knocker.

"How? In this thing, we stand out like fucking dog's bollocks—ah fuck!"

I looked ahead and saw what he did. I heard Wombat in the sleeper say, "Are you blokes going to stop fucking around soon?"

In my ear, I heard Cara. "Reaper, where are we going?"

"You'd better ask Michael Andretti that one," I replied.

"Who the fuck is he?" Knocker asked.

"You don't know?"

"No bloody idea, mate."

The truck crashed through the barriers and into the construction zone. The Scania's massive tires crushed them and sent debris flying. The van followed closely, dodging some falling scaffold and heavy machinery. The SUVs were still in hot pursuit and struggled to navigate the treacherous terrain, their tires skidding on loose gravel.

Suddenly one veered to the right, the driver losing control. The SUV plowed into a load of steel rods on a trailer, several lengths of which speared through the front window. I chose not to dwell on or imagine the resulting bloodbath.

The helicopter, now hovering dangerously low, unleashed a barrage of fire that tore through the construction site. Sparks flew as bullets struck metal beams and machinery. Knocker spotted an unfinished ramp and made a brave, if not stupid, decision. The truck accelerated.

"You'd better not be doing what I think you are," I shouted at him.

"Strap yourself in, Reaper. This is going to be fun."

"Fuck."

The truck launched off the ramp and crashed through a temporary fence, landing heavily on the other side. We seemed to bounce wildly, and how he never lost control is beyond me.

The van followed suit, its smaller frame making the jump with ease. The SUVs, however, were not as fortunate. One of the vehicles misjudged the jump, crashed into the ramp, and flipped over, ejecting its occupants as it came apart. The others struggled to regain control and smashed into each other.

The helicopter was circling back and unleashed another volley of gunfire. We were now back on the main road and swerved to avoid the deadly rain of bullets. Knocker spotted a narrow alleyway and made a sharp turn, and Holly followed closely. The alleyway was too tight for the truck, and I felt it shudder every time contact was made with the buildings on either side. "We're going to get stuck in here," I heard Kelly say.

The helicopter was still hovering above, waiting to get another crack at us, its spotlight sweeping the area. The truck and van emerged from the alley onto a deserted industrial area. Spotting an abandoned warehouse, Knocker made a beeline for it. Holly followed, both vehicles skidding to a halt inside the darkened building.

"What now, you pair of geniuses?" Cara asked over comms.

"Give us a minute, we're thinking." I glanced at Knocker. "Well?"

"Fucked if I know."

The helicopter circled above, its spotlight trying to illuminate the hidden vehicles. More SUVs had now regrouped and were approaching the area, obviously in comms contact with the rotored beast hovering above us. Inside the warehouse, we took a moment to catch our breath, knowing our pursuers would soon be upon us.

"You two gone to sleep?" Cara asked.

"Moments of intellectual brilliance take time," Knocker said in a low voice.

"Oh, please."

Looking around our temporary sanctuary, he noticed a stack of large, rusted barrels near the exit of the warehouse in front of us, the word *FLAMMABLE* illuminated by the headlamps. He looked at me, and we formulated a plan. Revving the truck's engine, Knocker charged forward, smashing into the barrels, sending them careering out into the open.

The helicopter, now directly above, hovered lower to get a better view. I leaned out the window and opened fire at the barrels as they rolled away.

My rounds hammered into them, and for a disappointing moment, I thought nothing was going to happen. Then, a massive explosion rocked the area. The barrels erupted in a fiery inferno, the shockwave sending the helicopter spiraling out of control. The pilot struggled to regain stability, but it was too late. The helicopter clipped the edge of the warehouse roof and crashed to the ground in a ball of flames.

Right in front of the incoming SUVs.

Suddenly, they were caught in the chaos and screeched to a halt, their occupants scrambling to avoid the debris. Now was our time, and taking advantage of the confusion, we sped out of the warehouse and disappeared into the night, leaving the burning wreckage behind. The chase was over, but the battle was far from won.

––––––––––––

We pulled over in a side street and checked the truck. One of the fuel tanks was leaking diesel all over the road from two holes in it. The van looked like a beehive, and so did the truck's trailer.

Cara and Holly joined us. Cara said, "The Atlas is hanging on, and the C-17 gun platform is still on station."

I nodded. "All we have to do is get to the airfield."

"Is the truck still operable?"

"It'll work," I replied.

"Then we'd best get going."

"Reaper One, copy?"

"Read you, Lima Charlie, Slick."

"You're not going to believe this."

"Try me," I shot back at him.

"You've got a tank heading your way, and you'll never believe the pace it's moving at."

I shook my head. "Yes, I would. It's that kind of evening."

The night was alive with the roar of engines, the screech of tires, and the rattle of gunfire once more. Our truck hammered through a roundabout, its trailer swaying dangerously, before straightening and Knocker's foot hitting the firewall once more. Close behind, Holly had the van sideways. We started weaving through traffic, Knocker glancing in the rearview mirror. The headlamps of three more black SUVs glinted menacingly, their occupants armed and ready. But the real threat was the T-14 Armata tank. Its turret swiveled, searching for us as it crushed everything in its path.

Knocker swerved sharply, narrowly avoiding a parked car. Holly and the van followed suit, its tires skidding on the damp pavement.

Not the tank though. It just crushed everything it saw as an impediment.

The SUVs closed in, the sound of their engines bouncing off the buildings on either side of the street.

One of them pulled forward alongside the van, a masked gunman leaning out of the window. He fired a burst of bullets, shattering the van's side window. In the truck's side mirror, I saw Cara fire her weapon through the window.

Then the van swerved violently, ramming the SUV into a lamppost. The vehicle crumpled on impact, but the following two SUVs came on undeterred.

The tank rumbled forward, its cannon firing a deafening shot. The shell exploded just behind the Scania's trailer, sending a shower of debris into the air. The trailer rocked violently, one of its rear tires blown off, but it remained on its wheels.

"Will someone do something about that fucking tank?" Knocker called out.

"Leopard One, copy?"

"Copy, Reaper One."

"We would really appreciate it if you could have a word to that tank on our six."

"We're working on it."

"Roger that."

"Satisfied?" I asked Knocker.

"No, I'm fucking not."

The truck swerved into another narrow street, our ever-present tails following. The tank, however, was too large for the alley, and plowed through a row of parked cars, its treads grinding metal and asphalt. The tank's cannon fired again, this time hitting a nearby building. The structure exploded in a shower of bricks and glass, debris raining down on the street.

"Motherfucker," Knocker growled.

"I'm thinking I should just walk," Wombat said dryly.

"I'll let you off at the next corner and you can take the fucking bus," Knocker said.

Now, after taking a few tight turns, the tank was starting to fall behind.

Knocker turned right again, and I heard Slick say, "Bad move."

"What?" I snapped back.

We found out why a few seconds later. Somehow, the tank had predicted our movements, and it burst through a building almost on top of us. It smashed into the trailer and separated it from the truck with violent force.

The trailer careered off, smashing into a row of parked cars and came to a halt in a cloud of dust and debris, car alarms calling out their plaintive wails. The truck, now lighter, sped ahead, Holly and the others in the van close behind.

The tank's turret turning, its cannon fired wildly. Another shell hit a building beside us, the explosion lighting up the night sky. The tank's crew barely had time to react before a new sound filled the air: incoming rounds from the gun platform above, the plane flying unbelievably low.

The gunship roared overhead, its cannons blazing. A storm of death rained down, tearing the plated behemoth apart. The explosion shattered the night in a fiery end to the armored beast.

All we had to worry about now was taking out the remaining SUVs.

And the motorbikes.

———

"You are fucking kidding me," I snarled as I looked into the side mirror.

"What is it?" Kelly demanded.

"You see them, Knocker?" I asked him.

"Yeah."

"I make it six."

"You could be right."

"Six what?" Kelly asked, effectively blinded to what was happening outside the truck by the sleeper cab.

"Motorbikes."

Each carried two people. The driver and the pillion was a shooter. I said into my comms, "Cara, we've got more company."

"I see them, Reaper. I think it's time we split up."

I nodded. "Do it. Good luck."

The van disappeared around a tight corner. The two SUVs still in the chase followed it. The bikes came on after us. I said, "Leopard One, track the van. Make sure it gets to the airfield."

"Roger that, Reaper One, will comply."

"You just told our aircover to piss off, Reaper," Knocker said loudly.

I grabbed the door handle and threw a wave at him. "That I did."

Then I climbed out of the cab.

I hooked around the rear of the cab and stood on the base of checker plate, which gave me solid footing. Reaching for the airlines, I hooked them around my left arm for more stability. Muttering to myself, I said, "Let's see what these assholes have planned."

I brought the MP5 up with one hand and fired a burst at the closest bike and rider. The bike weaved and almost crashed before the rider regained control. The shooter on the second bike opened fire, and bullets hammered into the cab around me.

Knocker swung on the wheel and took a left turn onto another street. Weightlessness suddenly took over and my feet left the plate I was standing on, walking on air as I became perpendicular to the truck's cab. I hung on for dear life as he straightened back up and gravity took over once more.

"You might want to warn me next time you make a fucking turn," I growled into my comms.

"Sorry, Reaper, forgot you were back there."

"Fucking pillock."

One of the bikes sped up, pulling alongside the rear wheels of the prime mover. The pillion shooter lifted a submachine gun to fire at me, but I managed to get off a burst before he could squeeze the trigger. Bullets struck home. The driver swerved slightly, but it was enough to send the bike crashing into a parked car.

The rider collided with the rear of the vehicle while the passenger was catapulted forward, sending him spearing headfirst into the car parked in front of it. Now I only had five more to worry about.

"Turn coming."

I readjusted my grip on the lines, holding tighter as the rear axles began locking up and the tires chirped on the damp asphalt. The nose of the prime mover came around, and the rear wheels commenced their slide. Once again, my feet came free of the aluminum deck, and had I lost my hold—like Wiley Coyote hitting the earth—there would have been a Reaper-shaped hole in the side of a building off to my left.

Back on a straight stretch again, I settled into a vertical position once more while Knocker's foot went down on the gas pedal. Dark black smoke poured from the stacks. The deep-throated growl of the truck reverberated from the surrounding buildings.

More gunfire from a nearby bike had me reconsidering the wisdom of leaving the relative safety of the cab. The thoughts were short-lived as I opened fire and the second rider and bike crashed. This time it just laid down and slid along the asphalt. The bike behind it, with nowhere to go, hammered straight into it, tossing both rider and passenger forward over the handlebars. They landed heavily on the road. Suddenly, I felt like a movie star from the '80s.

Now they tried a new tactic. Two bikes came at me. One on either side. They were going to hit me with a crossfire and there was nothing I could do about it. Except… "Knocker, hit the brakes."

He did it without hesitation and my back slammed against the cab's rear wall as we decelerated instantly. I grunted with the pain of it, but the two bikes shot past the front of the truck. Not quite so fortunate, the third bike plowed into the back of the chassis, the rider's head smashing into the turntable while the pillion was thrust directly at my head.

With only an instant to react, I dropped to my knees and the flying body hit headfirst into the back of the cab. The powerful diesel engines roared as Knocker accelerated again, and even above the noise, I was able to hear the sickening crack as the passenger's neck broke.

"Reaper, hang on."

I grabbed the airlines again, expecting a sharp turn.

Instead, the truck seemed to bounce and lurch across something, and then, from behind, I saw what it was. The mangled remains of a motorcycle, along with two lumps of chuck steak dressed in leathers, were regurgitated from beneath the speeding truck. "That will fuck your day up."

Then there was one.

The bike shot along ahead of us as the passenger fired back into the front of the truck. Knocker sped up, but the bike was too nimble, the rider swerving onto the sidewalk. For some crazy reason, Knocker tried to follow it and plowed into some parked cars before hooking back onto the street, leaving wailing car alarms in our wake.

"What the fuck was that, you lunatic?" I growled at my friend.

"Sorry, Reaper, lapse of judgment."

He shouted at me to hang on once more, and the truck changed directions. We had entered a street with festoon lights strung from building to building at that inconvenient height.

Becoming hooked on the twin exhaust stacks of the truck, with the forward momentum of the vehicle, they were consecutively pulled from their moorings, landing on the roof of the cab and hanging past my position. Electric sparks flashed and fizzed all around us. And here was I on the back and standing among it all, illuminated by a sea of deadly fireworks. "You're a fucking idiot."

"What are you complaining about now?" Knocker asked.

"You're trying to fucking kill me," I growled. "Any

minute now, I'll be lighting up like one of those street-lamps we just drove past."

"Yeah, sorry about that."

Bursting from the far end of the street, Knocker swung hard on the wheel, turning the Scania to the left. Just when I thought we might have been in the clear, the motorcycle reappeared. It was like an annoying mosquito in the dark of a night when you're trying to sleep. Only this one would kill you.

"Our friends are back," I said over my comms.

"Don't forget to say hello."

I brought the MP5 up and let loose another burst of fire. The bike came on, the bullets having no effect. I tried again. This time, the result was still the same. "Son of a bitch."

Leaning over the driver's shoulder, the passenger opened fire with what I think was a Mac 10. Once again, bullets hammered into the back of the cab, only this time, I think I felt one tug at the sleeve of my shirt.

Knocker put his foot down harder and the truck blew through an intersection. As chance would have it, the light was red.

"Hang on!" he shouted.

Once more, I was smashed into the rear of the cab from the impact. I remember looking to my left and seeing a Lada spinning away, all smashed up. I strug-gled back to my feet, wondering how long my luck could hold before I fell prey to my friend's driving prowess.

By now, I was on my knees. I swear I had bruises on my bruises. But here we were, driving through the streets of Volgograd in a smashed truck with people still trying to kill us.

"We have another intersection coming up," Knocker said.

I braced myself in preparation. With my luck, there'd likely be a semi blowing through it. Thank goodness I was wrong. It was only a garbage truck. And the motorcycle took the full force.

One minute, it was right behind us, following our passage. I was being shot at. Then the next, it had large truck wheels rattling across it. Metal and flesh became mingled as tons of garbage behemoth smashed into it.

I said, "That wrecked their night."

"Do you want to climb back in here now?" Knocker asked.

"Be right there."

Disengaging myself from the airlines, I sidled around the cab and opened the door. Returning to the passenger seat, I slammed the door behind me and took in my surroundings. "When did you renovate this place, Knocker?" I asked, noticing the extensive bullet damage. "Everyone okay?" All the occupants seemed to be unscathed.

"You're bleeding." It was Kelly who spoke. "Climb over here. I'll have a look at it."

Trading places with Wombat, I said, "Just don't treat me like Slick. It sounded like you were trying to murder him."

She ripped my shirt open to get a better look at the cuts. "I know one thing. He would have died a happy man."

———

Thirty minutes later we finally arrived at the airfield, finding the van already there. Holly and Cara opened their doors and stepped from the vehicle as we looked up to see the plane circling beyond our side. Holly ordered the Atlas to land for exfil. As we alighted from the damaged rig, Cara glanced at the truck. "Looking at that, I'm surprised anyone got out of it alive."

Knocker said, "I'm surprised that Tarzan here actually lived at all."

Holly frowned. "What do you mean?"

"He exaggerates too much," I told her.

Wombat looked at his boss. "You thought I was bad? But these two are a couple of crazy motherfuckers. What with him swinging off a truck like that, shooting everywhere."

"Who was hanging off the truck?" Cara asked.

"Reaper. Anybody would have thought he was trying out for Cirque de Soleil."

Both Holly and Cara frowned at me. I shrugged. "Like I said, they exaggerate. How far out is the plane?"

"Five minutes," Holly said.

"Fine, let's take those minutes and work out what the hell we're going to do now. We've got a nuke to find and no fucking idea where it is."

CHAPTER 8

THE ATLAS TOUCHED DOWN SMOOTHLY, AND WITHIN FIVE minutes, we were loaded and airborne again. Our main goal was to get out of Russian airspace before we were discovered and possibly shot down. I walked along the cargo hold to where Slick was operating. "What have you got?"

"I'm trying to find a train," he replied.

"What kind of train?"

"Anything that left Volgograd in the last couple of days. That might actually be useful to us," he replied. "Once I do, I'm going to reassign a satellite that has the capability of reading radiation. If we can find one that has the radiation reading, then we just might be able to get lucky. And I say might because I don't like our chances."

"Come on, Slick, where's your positivity?"

"I'm positive. All right, Reaper. Positive. We have a one in one thousand shot of finding it."

"To the one in a million."

"Wow, your support is overwhelming."

"Glad to be of service."

I left him to his work and crossed to where Cara was sitting. "How are you feeling?"

"Little stiff, little sore, but I put that down to Knocker's driving."

"Kelly said she patched you up while you were on the move."

"Yeah. She hasn't got a bad touch," I replied.

"She learned field medicine from the best."

"Brick?"

Cara nodded. "I had him do a full course with all the teams. Now, every time I have a team go out, nearly everyone knows enough combat medicine to keep people alive until help arrives."

"That's good."

"What are you going to do now, Reaper?"

"Find out where that super nuke went. Then stop it."

"Once we put down, I have to go back," she explained. "Duty calls and all that."

"It's been good to have your help," I told her.

"When are you coming back?"

"I think you've got it all handled without me."

Cara shook her head. "Maybe so, but it's not the same."

"Yeah."

Cara had us land in Poland. We were to take up residence outside of Warsaw at a black site the Brits used to conduct operations from. It was fully operational even after the threat of the Russian invasion.

Christine Ryan, somewhat unhappy about what had happened in Russia, met us there. The fact that we had missed the nuke and had Shatov within our grasp when he'd been killed compounded her displeasure.

Our small team was gathered in a briefing room complete with large screens and computers. Christine Ryan stood at the head of the table, glaring at us. Beside me, I heard Knocker say, "She looks like an old headmistress I once had at school."

"Shut the fuck up."

"Why do you suppose she's here?"

"You know I can hear you, right?" Christine Ryan said.

Knocker grinned. "Ah, you speak. I was starting to think you were an apparition."

"I'm in no mood for your bullshit, Mr. Jensen."

"Good. So why are you here?"

"Because of that crazy stunt you pulled in Volgograd."

Knocker looked at me. "Did you think that was a crazy stunt, Reaper? I don't think it was a crazy stunt. The pricks were waiting for us. They knew we were going to be there. And we barely got out with our lives."

I nodded. "Yes, I agree. It was a little bit close."

"When you two are finished fucking around," Christine Ryan growled.

"Are you done, Knocker?"

"Yes, Reaper, I do believe I am."

"Holly?"

"Don't bring me into your bullshit. Hang yourself if you want. I don't want anything to do with it."

"Okay," I said. "This is how it went. Shatov told us

about the Super nuke. We went to Volgograd, and it was a trap. And before you ask, no, I don't believe he set us up. Killing him would have been a senseless act had he been part of it."

"I see," mused Christine Ryan.

"Then they threw everything at us, including a tank. All designed to kill us and stop us from getting out of the city. However, we had backup."

"Yes, and you blew up half the city doing it."

"Small exaggeration. And it wasn't us who blew half the city up, it was the fucking tank."

"The Foreign Office isn't too happy about what happened," Ryan pointed out.

"Who gives a fuck," Knocker growled. "We're at war with them. The bastards are trying to blow up half of Europe. In my book, the mission is whatever it takes."

"Do you have to be so overt?"

"What?"

Christine Ryan picked up a remote and pointed it at one of the screens. Initially, the screen remained black, but when she pressed play, a feed of a truck rushing through the city while being chased by motorbikes appeared. Then the focus zoomed in on the back of the cab where a man stood holding on for dear life while firing an MP5.

"Anyone care to take a guess who that is?" she asked.

Knocker nodded, impressed. "Fuck, Reaper, you were busy back there."

"Yeah, hanging on. Some lunatic driver's trying to do everything he could to kill me."

"This is not funny," Christine Ryan snapped. "Your

fucking face is plastered all over Russian news services."

"Well fuck, I'm famous."

"You don't get it, do you?"

"I don't think you get it," I pointed out. "They knew we were coming. Yes, it might have been because of Shatov, but I don't think so. All of this is because of Hecate. The mole in our system. That is our problem."

"We've looked for the mole. We can't find your mole. Maybe this mole is in your head."

"Might I point out that we still have no idea who this mole is," Holland said. "You've been telling us it's been there for days, yet we've seen no proof. There have been no arrests."

Holly said, *"Whoever it is has been very good at covering their tracks. Just when we think we're getting close, they give us the slip or point us in the wrong direction."*

German said, *"So you're still no closer to finding out who Hecate is."*

I stared at him. *"That's right. For all we know, it could even be you."*

"I can assure you, Mr. Kane, I am not a Russian mole."

"I believe him, Reaper," Knocker said. *"I'm likely to think he's more of an asshole than anything else. Besides, he hasn't got the brains."*

German glared at Knocker. *"If this goes the way that I think, Mr. Jensen, I'm going to really enjoy locking you away. Hopefully, never to see sunlight again."*

"Do your best."

"Can we please continue?" Miriam asked.

I didn't buy that the mole was a figment of the

imagination. Everything pointed to there being one. However, we still needed to find the super nuke. "I'm thinking that you have an idea about what we should be doing, or you wouldn't be here."

"I'm taking you off it," Christine replied.

"Be fucked you are," I said defiantly.

"You have no say in the matter. I'm your boss, so what I say goes."

"Then you'll screw everything that we've worked toward."

"Hand everything you have to the new team. They will take over."

"It'll take days to catch them up, and by then, it'll be too late."

I looked at Knocker, who, for some reason, was holding back even though he looked as though he was about to lose his shit. Then I looked at Holly.

Who did lose her shit.

"This is fucking bullshit!" she shouted, leaping to her feet. "Absolute bollocks."

"Careful, Miss Smith," Christine Ryan cautioned her.

"Careful my fucking ass. After all the work we've put in, all the danger we've put ourselves through—"

"Sit down, Miss Smith."

"The fuck I will. You know just as well as I do that we don't have time to screw around here."

"Enough. There is a plane leaving for London tomorrow morning, Miss Smith. Be on it. Until then, you will brief the new team."

"Yes, ma'am."

Christine Ryan turned her attention to Slick,

Knocker, and me. "You three gentlemen can go home. Your services are no longer required."

"Just like that?"

"Just like that."

Then we were dismissed. But not done. Not by a long shot.

———

I made a call. We had checked into a hotel we'd been told to go to, leaving Holly to finish some reports at the black site.

The voice on the other end was soft and pleasant. "What do I owe the pleasure, John?"

"I have a problem that needs sorting," I told Anesha Perera.

"What might that be?" she asked.

I filled her in on what had happened and there was a moment of silence. "What is it you want me to do, John?"

"You're Home Secretary, Anesha, surely you can do something."

"I don't know what."

"Okay, let me lay this out for you so you understand. There is a nuclear weapon in play that has the capability of taking out a small country. We're being sidelined after all this time, and people who have no idea what they are dealing with are taking over. By the time they realize that, it'll be too late. Get us the hell back in the game, Anesha, or a lot of people are going to die."

"First, talk to me like that again, and I'll cut your bollocks off, John. Second, I have one thing I might be able to do. It is a Hail Mary, and I can't promise you anything."

"I'll take it."

"Leave it with me."

"Thanks, Anesha."

"Don't thank me yet."

The call disconnected and I knew it was now a matter of wait and see.

Knocker tossed me a beer. "Here. What did she say?"

"She is looking into it," I replied. I cracked the top and looked over at Slick. As usual, his face was buried in his computer screen. "Writing love letters to Kelly?"

He glanced up. "No, I finished them. You know, she is really flexible. I've never known a woman more flexible. She can—"

"TMI, Slick. I don't want to know," I said, cutting him off.

"I do," Knocker said, throwing the bottle top at me. "There's nothing on the idiot box."

"What are you doing, Slick?" I asked, ignoring my idiot friend.

"Trying to nail down a train," he replied.

"Didn't you hear?" Knocker said. "We've been given the ass."

"I don't care. I need to find that train," Slick replied.

"Why?"

"Because we're the only ones who can stop it," I said.

"Where do you figure it's at?" I asked him.

"I'm looking for a ghost train," Slick said.

"What's a ghost train?"

"America runs them all the time," he told me. "When they're shipping nuclear cargo and weapons. We all know the cartels would like to get their hands on the stuff. Basically, they're trains running on lines, with no record of them being there."

"How do they get through if no one knows they're there?" Knocker asked.

"I didn't say no one knew they were there, just that there was no record of them being there. They run them on a night and roster on certain operators who have passed classified training. Sorry, no pun intended. I'm thinking that the same happens in Europe."

"So how do you find them?"

"I run an algorithm to do with train stop and go signals. I start in Volgograd and see if it can pick up a pattern."

"And?"

"I'm still working on it."

Nodding, I walked to the balcony which jutted out from the Warsaw Hotel. It overlooked a street with lines of traffic moving like treacle, the honking of vehicle horns in symphony with sirens. The whole building's façade was sandstone and had a Victorian look about it.

It was big, boasting three function rooms, four gyms, and two restaurants. The owner was rumored to be an oilman from Saudi Arabia.

The thought of food made my stomach growl, and I decided that while we were able, we should be taking advantage of it. Returning inside, I said, "Are we dining out or in?"

Knocker had taken up position on the sofa. "Fuck it, I'm not moving."

"Slick?"

"Huh? Yeah."

I said, "I guess that's two. What about you, Reaper? Oh, I don't know. It's comfortable up here. Yeah, stuff it. We'll eat in the suite."

When neither responded, I muttered, "Hey, what do you want to eat?"

"Pizza," Knocker replied.

"Slick?"

"Yeah, pizza is good, Reaper."

So, that's what I ordered. For them. Hell, you should have seen their jaws drop when I sat down to a peppered steak with fries.

Around ten that night, Slick called out, excited, "I got it."

"The train?"

"I think so. I wasn't sure at first, but our ghost train isn't really a ghost train. More like a ghost carriage."

"You'd better explain."

"It took a little magic, but I nailed it down to a passenger train due to leave Minsk in Belarus tomorrow night at twenty-one hundred. It is quite unusual to have a train ready and waiting this far ahead of time. At the tail end of the train are two baggage cars."

"Okay."

Knocker said, "Yeah, I don't see it."

"I looked at the passenger manifest, and for the

number of passengers booked on the train, there is only need for one baggage car. Upon diving a little deeper, I came across this guy."

His screen changed to show a picture of a man wearing sunglasses, in his forties, and dressed for the Bahamas.

"Who is he?" I asked.

"Michel Fontaine. French mastermind in all things transportation. Him being booked on the train is a definite indicator that something significant is there. That guy doesn't get out of bed for anything less than fifty million."

"It doesn't mean that the package is on the train," Knocker pointed out.

I nodded. "Do we take the chance that it's not?"

"It's the best lead we have," Knocker replied.

"Don't you mean the only one we have? I'll reach out to Holly."

"Slow your roll, oh great scythe wielder," Knocker said. "You're not bringing the amateurs onboard?"

"No, but we need her. She's been with us from the get-go. Besides, she can get us tickets for the train."

"Fine, do it."

I grabbed my cell and made the call. Holly picked up on the second ring. "Can't sleep?" I asked her.

"Not really. What do you want?"

"Where are you? Are you back at the hotel yet?"

"Yes, I'm in my room."

"Get some clothes on and get in here now."

"Why?" she asked.

"Because I have something you might like to see."

The call was no sooner disconnected when another

came through. This one was Anesha. "Good, you're awake."

"We've been working on the problem. I think we might have come up with something," I told her.

"That is good because I have something too. There is a military intelligence team in Warsaw. No one knows either, except for you and a few select people. I'll send you the address. Be there tomorrow morning. The colonel in charge is expecting you."

"Can they get us what we want?"

"They have been told to take care of you."

"Thanks."

"Good luck."

Holly arrived a few moments later, after all, she was in the suite next door. "What do you have?"

I gave her a brief rundown, then Slick told her more.

"Shit, what I'd give for some backup about now," she moaned.

"Don't worry, I took care of that too."

"What do you mean?"

I told her.

"Shit, Christine is going to fucking wig."

"Anesha sent me an address."

"Where?"

I shook my head. "Haven't had—"

The lights went out.

CHAPTER 9

Now accustomed to unusual occurrences, my hand went to my Glock just as the backup power came on. The lighting was dim but enough for us to see. The elevators would be off-line, as well as other things throughout the hotel. "This can't be good."

Knocker said, "No prizes for guessing what's going on."

"We need to get out...now."

"Remind me to shoot the fucking mole in the head whenever we find them, Reaper."

We started for the door. Holly said, "I'm not armed."

I said, "Forget it. If you need one, I'm sure we can—"

"Here," Slick said, giving her his own Glock along with his spare magazines. "I'll take care of the computer."

The hallway was clear. I guess the hour being after ten helped that somewhat. Leaving our room, we followed the corridor toward the elevators, pressing the button when I reached it, wanting to confirm what I already knew. They weren't working.

The shrill squeak of the stairwell door made us stop and turn.

For a moment, we were stuck in the open, but to our right was another cross hallway, which we scrambled into. I waited for a moment, peering around the corner. They appeared moments later. Four men, weapons out in the open.

I drew back from the corner to evade detection and followed the others to inform them of the threat. Moving back to the same position, I waited to see what the intruders would do. They walked past. Using hand signals, I indicated for Knocker to keep moving. We followed the parallel hallway back to the stairwell. Knocker grabbed the door and swung it open before I could stop him. The familiar screech seemed deafening in the silence. "What the fuck, dickhead?" I growled in a low whisper.

"What the fuck yourself."

"Just get going."

Heading down, we made it to the second floor before an encore performance of the door above and the clang of another below made us stop. Then came Russian voices punctuated by radio traffic. I pointed to the door beside us. "In there."

Knocker opened the door, this one substantially better maintained and quieter, and found it clear on the other side. We sprinted down the corridor until we found another cross hallway. Pausing there, Holly took out her cell. "I'll call Ryan."

She punched in a number, frowned, and shook her head. "Maybe not. Everything is jammed."

"You can bet they'll have this place locked down and start searching it floor by floor soon," Knocker said.

"I'd like to know what we're dealing with," I said.

"Maybe we could use a room phone," Holly said.

"Everything will go through the switch," I told her.

"Worth a try."

"Fine, let's wake someone up." I looked at the door across from us. "Here is good."

I banged on the door and waited.

A few moments later, I heard, "Yes, who's there?"

The voice was American, sounded elderly. A woman.

"Fire department."

This time it was Holly who gave me a what the fuck look. I shrugged my shoulders. Unexpectedly, the door opened by an elderly woman with almost white hair and wearing a floral robe. "Who are you, asshole?" she growled in her sternest voice.

I loved her already. "Ma'am, if we can come in, I'll explain everything."

"You a Marine son?"

I shook my head, trying to figure her out. "Was, ma'am."

"I knew it. My Frank was a Marine too. I can tell."

"Can we come in, ma'am?"

"You ain't going to mug me, are you?"

"No, ma'am."

She stepped aside. "Come on in then."

We filed into the room and closed the door behind us. The old woman gave us all a stern look and said, "Don't make too much noise, you'll wake my Frank up. He's not as young as he used to be."

"We'll be as quiet as we can, ma'am."

"Alice," she said. "My name is Alice."

"Hi, Alice, I'm John. This is Holly, Sam, and Raymond."

Knocker glared at me. Alice smiled. "Such nice names. I like Raymond very much."

"Call me—"

"Call him Ray, Alice. He likes that."

"Nonsense. Raymond sounds so much better."

My grin broadened. I couldn't help it. "Yes, ma'am, it certainly does."

"Now, what are you young people up to?"

"Would it be possible to use your room phone, Alice?" Holly asked. "There is a situation, and we need to resolve it."

The old woman frowned. "What's wrong with your room phone?"

"Raymond broke it, ma'am."

Knocker glared at me. Alice turned to him and said with a scolding tone, "You should be more careful with things that aren't yours, young man."

"It was an accident, ma'am. I promise I'll be more careful from now on."

"Oh, you're British. You sound like James Bond. Very dapper."

Holly picked up the phone's receiver and waited. I walked over to the large window with a view of the street but saw nothing. Turning back, Holly had hung up the phone. "Nothing."

"Slick?"

"The only way is to get to the switch," he replied.

"Where is that?" I asked.

"Front desk."

"Can't you do anything?" Knocker asked.

"No, I'm even locked out of the CCTV. I can try to get back in, but I can't say if or when."

Alice clapped her hands. "Oh, my, this sounds... did any of you watch that British show, Spooks?"

"Raymond was in it, ma'am," I lied.

"Oh, really?"

"Season Four, Alice. Rewatch it, you'll see him."

"Which episode—oh..."

Knocker had drawn his Glock and was walking toward the door. "Come on, Reaper, let's go make that fucking call."

Alice held up a fist. "You go fuck their ass, Raymond."

He spun around, a pained expression on his face. "It's kick, Alice. Kick their ass."

A look of disappointment came across her face. "Oh, yes, sorry."

I grinned and followed him out the door.

The hallway was clear as we made our way toward the stairwell. About halfway there, I stopped and looked at the emergency fire alarm. Knocker said, "What are you doing?"

I nodded to the small red box. He stared at it and said, "Try it."

So I did. And nothing happened.

"They've disabled it," Knocker growled in a low voice.

"Back to plan A then."

We were almost back at the stairwell when the door opened and two armed men appeared. Immediately, our weapons came up and crashed loudly. Both shooters dropped with three rounds in their chests.

"Bollocks," Knocker moaned. "That'll bring the bastards running."

Behind us, a room door opened, and a man appeared, his attention drawn by the noise of the shots. "Get back in your room," I shouted at him.

He vanished as fast as he'd appeared. I looked down at the dead men in front of us. Knocker gave them a quick check. Their tattoos told us all we needed to know. "Igoshin's people."

I nodded. "I'm sick of these pricks finding us all the time."

"Maybe now that we're detached from MI6, we might be able to turn the tables."

"I guess we'll find out."

Both dead mercenaries were armed with Czech-made suppressed CZ Scorpion Evo 3s. We picked them up and took some spare magazines with us. Then we went into the stairwell and started down.

On the ground floor, Knocker eased the door open a crack to peer out into the reception area of the hotel. Using his hand, he indicated three tangos in the immediate area. Two to the right, one to the left. Then he signaled that he would go right. Three fingers up, and the countdown began.

As soon as his hand became a fist, Knocker hit the door and burst through. His first target took rounds and fell before they became aware of our presence. The second turned to face us, trying to bring their weapon into line, and died almost as fast.

As soon as Knocker had cleared my line of fire, I had my own weapon up and working. The shooter on the left was already moving, lifting his gun to shoot at my friend, but both my shots caught him dead center, preventing him from pulling his trigger. He fell to the hard floor and blood started to pool around him.

Knocker pushed forward in the direction of the main desk. I was right behind him when another mercenary appeared from behind a pillar, firing his weapon.

"Christ!" Knocker exclaimed.

He threw himself behind a sofa in the foyer. Bullets chewed through the fabric and foam. The shooter was so intent on his target that he failed to see me. His mistake.

A couple of well-placed shots sent him to join his friends in mercenary hell.

Sweeping the rest of the area, we found it clear but stepped toward a body when a radio came to life with a loud crackle. Knocker listened intently for a moment and then looked over at me.

"They've found the dead ones we left behind. They're calling everyone to see what's left."

The radio crackled again. "They're calling in reinforcements, Reaper. We need to get the fuck out of here before we're stuck."

"We can't leave everyone behind," I told him, meaning all the hotel guests.

"It's us they want, not them," he pointed out.

"Yeah, but how many are going to get hurt while they're looking. See if you can make the call."

Knocker hurried over to the desk and started to fiddle around. In the end, he threw his arms up in disgust and said, "Nope, it's fucked. They must be jamming it all somewhere else."

I thought for a moment and then it struck me. "There was a removal truck across the street."

Knocker raised his eyebrows. "This time of night?"

"Let's take a look."

We hurried toward the front doors and found them chained. Knocker muttered a curse and said, stand back. He fired two shots into the floor-to-ceiling window beside them and glass cascaded in a razor-sharp waterfall. He stepped through, glass crunching beneath his boots. I quickly followed, and we approached the truck as best we could without being seen.

Knocker grabbed the door handle and reefed it open without hesitation. Two heads swung toward us, surprised expressions on their faces. Our eyes locked, and I fired, sending a mist of blood coating parts of the cab's interior. They slipped from their positions and fell to the floor between the seats.

Knocker and I climbed in and closed the door behind us. I said, "See what you can find."

We both started looking around but found nothing. Knocker said, "This is a bloody Slick thing."

"Yeah."

We continued to search, hoping that we'd missed something the first time. Finally, I said, "Fuck it. Let's go to plan B."

"What's plan B?"

"Kill them all."

"Hell, I'm all for that, but we have no idea how many there are. Wait, I have an idea."

Knocker picked up the radio and said, "Hey, assholes, are you listening?"

Several seconds elapsed before the radio crackled to life. "Who is this?"

Knocker said, "I was just walking past your truck

and I could hear something ticking. It could be a bomb."

"Who is this?" the voice demanded again.

Placing the radio receiver on the dash, Knocker's hand went into one of his pockets. When he pulled it out, he held up a fragmentation grenade. I shook my head. "Christ, Knocker."

"You might want to get out, Reaper."

I opened the rear door, and we both scrambled out. Knocker pulled the pin on the grenade and threw it back into the truck. "Run."

The detonation of the grenade caused a secondary explosion and the truck became engulfed in orange flames. Knocker nodded happily and said, "That'll bring them running."

So, we took up position behind a raised garden bed and waited. Not very long, mind you. In under a minute, the remaining shooters began tumbling out through the broken window and into a raging crossfire.

There were six of them. Most fell within moments of emerging. After the first assault, two remained but were so shocked by what happened to their friends that they threw down their weapons.

Knocker and I stepped from our positions of cover and closed in on them. "Get on your knees," I snarled.

The pair fell to their knees and automatically placed their hands behind their heads. "Who sent you?"

As expected, they said nothing.

"Do you work for Igoshin?"

Still nothing.

"Okay, we don't have much time before—"

Many of the hotel guests began emerging from the shattered glass window, looking around in stunned amazement.

Knocker fired several shots into the air to get their attention then yelled, "Piss off inside!"

His actions elicited a few yelps, and the guests melted back into the hotel. Knocker said, "Someone will be filming this, bet your ass they will be."

"Worry about that later."

As it turned out, we made the six a.m. news. I turned my attention back to the two mercenaries. "We don't have much time, so the one who talks first doesn't get a bullet in the head. Where is Igoshin?"

Nothing.

"Knocker."

He raised his Glock.

"Wait!" the man on the left exclaimed. "Grigori is with a special team."

"What special team?"

"I do not know. We were told nothing."

"How did you know we were here?" I asked.

"We received a call," the second man said.

"Who from?"

"I don't know. We were told you would be here and the room you were in."

I nodded slowly. "Was it Hecate?"

The one on the left shook his head, unsure. The other nodded. "I think that is what Hans said."

"Who is Hans?"

"Our team leader. He was German."

"Was?"

The man on the right nodded at one of the bodies. "That is him."

The wail of sirens could now be heard in the background. "Is Igoshin with the nuke?"

"I don't know."

There didn't appear to be anything more to be gained from them, so I growled, "Get out of here."

They didn't need telling twice, scrambling to their feet and racing off into the darkness to put as much distance between themselves and the fast approaching sirens. I looked at Knocker. "We'd better do the same."

―――――

Arriving on the doorstep of the military intelligence house at a little after seven, we were greeted and let in by a corporal named Darcy: a slender woman with a sleeve tattoo on her left arm, her head almost completely shaved.

She took us through to meet the colonel in charge. His name was Owen Fletcher-Jones. He was a man of great disposition. All of it less than sunny. "Are you people going to cause me trouble?" he asked.

"Depends," replied Knocker before we could say anything.

The colonel's eyes narrowed. His handlebar mustache twitched. "On what, son?"

"He means no," Holly interjected, stepping forward.

Fletcher-Jones's gaze switched over to her. "Who might you be?"

"Holly Smith, MI6. Soon to be out of a job, I expect."

He looked at me. "You?"

"John Kane. I'm nobody."

"A nobody I do believe I've heard of. Now, why have you been forced upon me?"

Holly's cell buzzed. She looked at it and rejected the call. Fletcher-Jones looked irritated. "Do you need to take that, Miss Smith?"

"No, it's my old boss."

"Fine. Somebody fill me in. Wait, I almost forgot." He stared at Slick. "Who are you?"

"I'm the computer nerd," Slick replied.

"Uh, huh. Okay, why are you here?"

"We need a base of operations," Holly said. "Somewhere we can set up and track down a device that could blow the shit out of half of Europe."

"Sounds important," the colonel said, his face showing no reaction to the news. "Where is this device?"

"On a train in Minsk, one we need to get on."

"And you need military intelligence to get you to Minsk and give you backup should the need arise, right?"

"If possible," Holly replied.

"We'll see what we can do."

"Thank you, sir."

CHAPTER 10

MINSK RAIL STATION WAS BUSY. THE COLONEL AND HIS people had successfully inserted us into the city, and we were now ready to leave on the train. We'd left Slick in Warsaw so he could weave his magic from there. Somewhere, however, among the preparations, Christine Ryan had discovered what we were doing and made a last-minute attempt to bring us back in under her umbrella so she could sideline us and use a different team.

When she couldn't, she used her team anyway. We picked them out on the platform just before we boarded. "Eleven o'clock," I whispered into my comms.

"Another at six," Holly said.

"I've got two more," Knocker replied.

"So that's four."

"Five," Holly said. "Three guys, two women."

I said, "How did they find out what we were up to?"

I heard Holly say over the comms, "Bravo to Alpha, copy?"

"Copy, Bravo," Fletcher-Jones replied.

"Do you have any idea how Six found out about our op?"

"That would be from me, Bravo. I received a phone call."

"Shit."

"Say again?"

"We have a second team on mission, Alpha," Holly said.

"The more the merrier."

"Be fucked," Knocker growled. "They just increased the chances of a fuckup."

"Heads up," Slick said, breaking into the transmission. "Fontaine is coming toward you on your six, Bravo One. He has two riders with him."

Turning slightly, I looked back and noticed Fontaine the Frenchman, his riders following closely. The riders were tall, with athletic bodies, their dark hair cut in a pixie style. One wore a short green dress, the other had settled on blue. Both wore long overcoats, and for a moment, I thought I saw the outline of a hidden weapon.

"Any ID, Slick?"

"Sonia and Louisa Thomis," he replied.

"Who are they?" Holly asked.

"Former Air Parachute Commando. Combat Search and Rescue. They do sound tough."

I watched them get on the train. I said, "Okay, head on a swivel. There will be more than just them on the train."

"Reaper, our friends are moving," Knocker said.

"Let's hope they don't fuck everything up."

"You want us to get on?"

I looked at my watch. "Not yet, let's see what happens."

So, we stayed where we were, watching passengers saying their goodbyes to friends and family before boarding the train. Nothing specific stood out to us until we saw Fontaine and the Thomis sisters disembark the train.

I said, "Alpha, something isn't right. They just got off the train again."

"Why would they do that?" Holly asked.

"Don't know. Let's follow them."

We each took up positions where we could see and follow at a safe distance. They went up a set of stairs and then crossed over to a secondary platform. It was there they got onto another train.

"Slick, did you get that?"

"Roger. I'm checking it out."

"Where is it going?"

"Wait one."

The public address system made an announcement about a train leaving and gave the platform number. It was then that I realized we were on that very one. "Slick, I need that intel."

"Working on it."

"Fuck it. Get on the train."

"No, wait. I don't—"

But it was too late, we were on it. And the train was pulling away.

"We're going to need some electronic tickets," Holly said.

"Working the problem, ma'am," Slick replied.

"Now, Slick," I said, staring at the conductor coming our way in the carriage hallway.

He reached Knocker first. "Sir, are you all right?"

"What?" Knocker asked, playing dumb.

"Are you having trouble, sir? Finding your cabin?"

"Ah, maybe just a little bit," Knocker replied.

"Show me your ticket, sir, and I will be able to help you."

"Slick, you need to make this happen," I said under my breath.

"I'm trying, Reaper."

Knocker patted his pockets. "Ticket, ticket, where did I put it?"

"Could it be on your phone, sir?" the conductor asked.

A stupid grin appeared on Knocker's face. "Yes, my phone."

"Slick?"

"It's on the way, Reaper."

I heard Knocker's cell ding as he pulled it from his pocket. He looked at the screen and smiled at the conductor. "Here it is."

He showed the conductor, who returned his smile and said, "Right behind you, sir."

"Oh?" Knocker turned. "Oh, okay. Thank you."

Then the conductor turned to Holly and me. "Sir? Madam?"

I reached for my cell. Slick had come through. He looked at the e-ticket and said, "Yes, the double suite. Next door to this one."

"Sorry, Reaper, it was the best I could do on short notice."

The conductor moved away, leaving us to sort

ourselves out. All three of us entered the suite. It was small, but for two people, it would have been comfortable enough. "Slick, tell me about the train."

"It is routed to Paris via Berlin. Ten passenger cars, two dining cars, sleeping cars, and—"

"What?"

"We have an extra at the rear. Looks to be a vehicle transport car."

"Open or closed?"

"Open."

"You figure that it could be in one of them, Reaper?" Knocker asked.

"Possible."

Holly said, "Slick, run an ID package through the passengers and see if anything pops. I'd like to know who doesn't belong. And check on our friends. Find out where they are."

With a sudden jerk, the train set out and we were away on our journey.

————

Sitting comfortably in the suite car, we worked out a tentative plan of action. Until Slick gave us a relatively accurate picture, we didn't know what we were facing. "Who's for a beer?" Knocker asked.

I stood up. "One won't hurt. I'm curious to have a look around anyway."

We headed down to the dining car, a small bar inside the door. The bar attendant was an attractive woman with blonde hair pulled back into a ponytail. "What can I get you, sir?"

"Three beers."

She capped three bottles of Heineken before placing them on the polished counter in front of us, then turned to gather some frosty glasses. I held up my hand and said, "The bottles will do."

"As you wish."

I held out twenty euros, but she declined. "The cost is covered in the price of the ticket."

"Thank you."

The dining car was empty, so we had our choice of seats. We selected a table mid-carriage. "Reaper, there might be an issue," Slick said in my ear.

Knocker looked at me. "Just tell him to shut up. Every time he says *might*, he really means there is, and we almost get killed."

"Speak to me, Doom Sayer."

"Fuck," Knocker muttered.

"Look around you and tell me what you see," Slick said.

"No one."

"That is pretty much what it is like through the length of the train."

"Are you saying this is a ghost train?" I asked.

"Almost. The main concentration of people is in cars two and four, with three people in car three."

"So, we have to go through carriage four to get to our target, is that what you're saying?"

"Affirmative."

"That means that two and four would be armed bodyguards," Holly said.

"How many passengers in two and four, Slick?"

"Ten in each."

"And there it is," Knocker growled. "A good old

fuck you mixed in with a double-loaded shit sandwich."

"Over the top or underneath," I replied.

"What?"

"We go over the top to get to him or underneath."

Knocker said, "I vote over the top."

I looked at Holly. "You go to the car transport and see what you can find."

She nodded. Then she asked, "What about our bartender?"

I stared at the woman behind the bar. Holly was right. It was an even money bet that she was one of Fontaine's people. "We'll head back to our carriage first and go from there."

"There is also the conductor," Knocker said.

With a shake of my head, I said, "No, not him. He isn't the right fit."

"Okay, let's do it that way."

We left our beers and got up from the table, making our way back past the bar. The bartender asked, "Will there be anything else?"

"No, we're fine, thank you," Holly said.

Back in the suite, I grabbed a small Geiger counter, which I handed to Holly. "You got your weapon?"

"Yes."

"Okay." I dug into a small compartment of my backpack and took out three suppressors. "Here."

Attaching them to our weapons, we performed a comms check, and then we were ready. I stuck my head out the door to see if the coast was clear and saw two men coming along the hallway. I ducked back inside and closed the door. Turning to the others, I held my forefinger to my lips in the universal signal for silence. In my ear, I heard Slick say, "They're slowing, Reaper."

The suppressed Glock came up, and I pointed it at the closed door. Then Slick said, "They're outside the second room. Weapons are out."

I heard the door of the cabin beside us open, followed by voices.

"They're confused."

We waited, expecting them to open the suite door. But instead, they went away. "Where are they going, Slick?" I asked.

"Back the way they came."

"Fuck it."

I opened the door and stepped out into the hallway. My Glock was shoulder high and I fired twice at the first target and then twice at the second. They each let out a grunt of pain and fell forward.

Striding forward, I grabbed the one closest to me and dragged him back toward the cabin they had just searched, the one allocated to Knocker. I dumped him inside and stepped aside as Knocker brought the second body.

"Right, time to move."

Closing our door behind us, we began making our way toward the rear of the carriage. In line with the last cabin, we separated, Knocker and I went inside while Holly continued going toward the car carrier.

We were not at all surprised to find the cabin empty. Upon checking the window, I saw that it was a sealed, one-piece unit. Bringing up the Glock, I fired twice. The window shattered, and I cleared the remaining glass from the opening. The passing landscape was roaring by outside, and the wind began buffeting the interior. Tucking the Glock inside my pants, I said, "Hold my beer."

"I'm glad you're going first, Reaper," Knocker said. "That way, if you die, I can see what you screwed up and learn from your mistake."

"You're such a great friend."

"No, I'm not, I'm just smarter."

Grabbing the edge of the opening, I started to climb. Once outside the carriage, there wasn't much to hold onto, and for a moment, I felt like a cowboy in an old western movie. Except this was real and the train was going a lot faster.

I found a handhold and dragged myself toward the roof of the carriage. My boots scrambled for purchase, but I had trouble finding something to hook onto. Finally, I got what I needed and pushed my way up further. I found another handhold and moved over the curved edge until I felt more secure. Now that I was on top, I rolled over and closed my eyes. "Okay, Knocker, your turn."

I rolled back over toward the edge and leaned down so I could see him climb. He came out through the opening and started to come up. Once he was in the right position, I grabbed him and pulled him up top.

We lay there for a moment and then something occurred to Knocker, who said, "How are we going to get inside the carriage?"

"What do you mean?"

Making sure it was safe to do so, he sat up. "Look where the carriages meet. It's not like the old days, mate. There is no way in."

"Shit. Let's take a look."

He was right. There was no way down. I shook my head. After a moment, I said, "Slick, copy?"

"Roger."

"Can you see us?"

"Affirmative," he replied.

"If we climb down, are you able to open the entry doors to give us access?"

"Wait one." A minute later, he said, "Roger that."

"We need to get to the right carriage before we go busting in. Give us a little time to get into position."

"Copy."

We made steady progress across the train roof, making it to the carriage we needed to get to. To get back down, we had to reverse our actions and take up our positions over the doorway for the perilous maneuver. I slid down, hanging precariously onto the side of the carriage. Moments later, Knocker joined me. "Open it, Slick."

When the door slid open, we both swung in, landing in a small, concealed vestibule with an internal door that entered the main carriage. This one was a lounge car and, supposedly, where we would find Fontaine.

What we weren't expecting was that he was there with Louisa Thomis. Of her sister, there was no sign. Not then, anyway.

We entered the carriage with weapons raised. A glass of champagne in his hand, Fontaine was seated opposite Louisa Thomis. She also had a glass. The transporter looked up at us and said, "Hecate said you would come."

There it was, the bane of our current existence.

"You wouldn't by any chance have a name, would you?"

He smiled and saluted me with the wine glass. Louisa put down her glass and rose to her feet, moving to relieve us of our weapons and comms.

Behind us, the door opened, and Sonia Thomis appeared with Holly. Holly shrugged. "If it's any consolation, I didn't find anything."

"Ha, of course you didn't," Fontaine burst out with more than a hint of glee. "Do you think I would be stupid enough to lead you straight to the item when I knew you were coming?"

"One could hope," Knocker replied.

"So where is it?"

The grin stayed on his face. "It is safe."

"What's the target?"

"Would you like a drink? We have wine, beer, water."

"Sure, why not? Beer will be fine. Might as well squeeze one in before you kill us."

Fontaine looked at Knocker. "What about you?"

In typical Knocker style, he said, "I suppose that a go around the bedroom with the twins wouldn't be out of the question? I mean, after all, if a man's going to die, he might as well die happy."

"Shall we let them decide?" Fontaine said.

He looked at the twins. Their faces were masks of hatred. Knocker said, "Yeah, I don't think that's going to happen. I'll settle for the beer."

"Miss Smith?"

"Sure."

Suddenly, I was curious. "You know what you're transporting, right?"

"I do not ask my customers such questions. All I am hired to do is transport the package from point A to point B."

"So you don't know?" I asked to confirm.

"That is what I just said."

Knocker said, "I think he needs to start up a new line of business, Reaper. Oops, yeah, that's not going to happen. He'll be dead."

I nodded. "Too true."

"What are you people raving on about?"

I glanced at Holly. "Do you want to tell him? I mean, I can, but I think it would be better coming from you."

"Are you sure?"

"Yes, in my experience, women always seem to deliver bad news the best."

"Okay, if you insist."

Fontaine was getting angry. "Will one of you tell me what the hell you're talking about?"

"You are transporting a nuclear device. But not just any type of nuclear device. This one's big enough to wipe out a small country."

The Frenchman stared at her. Knocker saw the concern on his face. "That's right, Frenchy, kiss your ass goodbye."

I said, "Sometimes it pays to ask what you might be transporting. Wouldn't you agree?"

"You are lying."

"I wish I was. So, let me give you a quick rundown. You are transporting the nuclear device for someone named Genady Morozov. The guy is Russian. Back in the day, he was a general in the Russian army. Now he's just a sick fuck who's trying to work his way into immortality. There were five of them called The Gods of War. Someone back in the early Cold War days came up with a plan. If ever the West became a threat, then they would fight back. The nuclear weapon was part of it. The plan has been in the making for years. Sergey Lash was one of the ones behind it as well. Once he came to power, it was then put into motion. The ultimate goal is to put all the USSR back together. But we kind of foiled that. Now they're going to detonate their bomb. We just don't know where or when."

Fontaine wanted not to believe it, but he couldn't get past the fact that he knew it was true. I just needed something else to push him over the edge.

I said, "They will have their own people escorting it. My guess is Grigor Igoshin. He's a Russian mercenary, if you haven't heard. He'll have his people guarding it as well. I also think that nobody is meant to come back alive. But Igoshin will be the only one who knows that. How about you tell us where that bomb is?"

"It is on a ship."

"Where?"

"The Black—"

BANG!

My head whipped up and I saw Louisa standing with her sidearm out and pointing at Fontaine. Her dark eyes flicked to me. "They said he would fold if he found out."

"I would have said he didn't want to die. Obviously, you have no such problem."

"South America will be a long way from the blast zone," she replied.

"This was all just a trap?" Holly asked.

"Yes, to be rid of you once and for all," Sonia said.

"Where to from here?" I asked.

"You will be taken from the train at the next station and driven somewhere to be shot. That is all."

"And you?"

"We have a plane to catch."

I shrugged. "Okay, well, how about that beer?"

CHAPTER 11

I HAD ALMOST FINISHED MY BEER WHEN WE FELT THE train begin to slow. Louisa Thomis sat across the table from me, her Glock pointed at my chest. She said, "This is it. The conversation was stimulating."

The sarcasm was evident. In reality, we'd not exchanged two words but had stared across the table in silence.

When I got to my feet, the others followed suit. As we left the train, we were escorted by five armed guards. The platform was old and run down, the station house barely used. Maybe one day it would be sold off and repurposed as a museum, but until then, it was just a derelict shell.

A canvas-covered truck lay waiting for us behind the station, and we were escorted to the rear bed and made to climb in. As I sat down, a cheerful face peered at me over the tailgate. It was Louisa. "It is a shame that we did not get time to talk more. I'm sure under different circumstances we could have become quite good friends. Guns in the bed sheets and all that."

I just shrugged my shoulders. There wasn't much left to say. She disappeared from the rear of the truck, and I heard her shoes crunch on the gravel as she approached the cab. I looked up as three armed guards climbed into the back of the truck with us. Then I heard her voice say, "Take them away. Deep into the forest. I don't want their bodies ever to be found."

The truck growled deeply as we pulled away from the train station. The road was narrow, and what asphalt was there was full of holes. As I watched the landscape trundle by over the tailgate, I could see where we had once been but not where we were going. The three guards' faces remained stoic.

Half an hour after leaving the train station, we turned onto a dirt road in among a large pine forest. The driver worked down through the gears as he made the turn. The rear of the truck rocked violently as he hit a hole. We heard the gearbox grind once more as he changed down another gear, and then his foot mashed the gas pedal and the truck lurched forward. The trees around us became thicker and overhead it grew darker. When we eventually reached a clearing, the truck made a half-turn before jerking to a stop. "Well, I guess this is it."

Our three guards climbed from the back of the truck then turned to face us, indicating that they wanted us to follow them. The ground beneath our feet was damp, probably due to the limited sunlight filtering through the tops of the pines. The trunks on the trees were arrow-straight as they all fought to find sunlight at the top of the canopy. The driver and the passenger walked to the back of the truck, joining our small group. One of our guards pointed through the trees and said, "Go that way."

"What if I don't want to?" asked Knocker.

A guard to his left stepped in beside him and hit him behind the ear with a handgun. Knocker buckled at the knees and went down, placing his hand on the ground to steady himself. He looked up at his assailant, his eyes narrowed and he said, "You fucking pillock."

The guard went to hit him again. I stepped forward and grabbed him by the arm. "Leave him."

So he hit me instead. A sweeping backhand blow that caught me up the side of the head. I went to my knees, side by side with Knocker. He looked at me and gave a wry grin. "You okay, Reaper?"

"Remind me never to help you again. It bloody hurts."

"Not as much as this is going to," he replied with a grin and came up swinging.

Knocker's fist was full of knife. His arm swept in a deadly arc, the blade he'd taken from his boot slicing through the fleshy throat of the nearest guard. The man lurched back as a bright spray of warm blood spurted from his carotid artery.

The would-be executioner staggered then fell, his hand trying to stem the flow of blood. Knocker's movements were explosive. His muscular arm came around and he whipped his wrist down and released the knife. It tumbled through the air before burying deep into the chest of the second executioner. The third guard beside me brought up his arm to shoot Knocker, but I drove my shoulder in under his rib cage and knocked him sprawling sideways. Before he knew what was happening, I was on top of him, my fist pounding three times. My other hand was locked onto the wrist holding the gun. Each blow jarred up through my arm and into my shoulder. When I stopped, his face was bloody and there was no movement. Three down, two to go.

Holly had reacted instantly. She let go with a back hand left chop across the throat of the guy who'd traveled in the passenger seat up front. He'd been distracted by the commotion and was trying to shoot us without wounding or killing his friends when she'd acted.

He grabbed his throat, his jaw opening wide as he tried to gasp in breath. Holly grabbed for the gun hand and twisted savagely, breaking the finger so he'd release it. With fluid movements, the gun came up, pressed against the side of his head, and she pulled the trigger. His head snapped to the side and his legs gave out as though he was a marionette with the strings cut.

Holly pivoted. The gun snapped into line with the final shooter, the driver, and she squeezed the trigger just as he fired his own weapon. Her bullet flew true and smashed into the side of his head. His bullet, however, tugged at the fabric of Knocker's jacket and went screaming off into the forest.

Silence descended over the forest. This part of our ordeal was over. I drew several breaths deep into my lungs and looked around. I turned to check that Holly was okay, then my eyes settled on Knocker.

I said, "Next time you want to do something like that, how about you let me know first?"

"Sorry, Reaper didn't have time."

I walked over to the truck and looked at the ignition. There were no keys. "Knocker, check them for the truck keys."

"Roger that."

Holly walked over to me. "This is getting beyond a joke, John. Someone keeps giving up our movements. It won't be much longer before one of us, if not all, is going to be killed."

"Yes, our cat lives are running out fast."

"Before Fontaine was shot, he was going to say Black Sea, wasn't he?"

I nodded. "That would be my guess. From there, out through into the Med."

"We assumed that the target was going to be Paris. But if they've changed it, they could be headed anywhere. They could sail it into the bloody Thames if they wanted to."

My face was grim. "We need to find that ship."

———

It took us three days to locate the ship, and by then, it was out in the Med. Not that that was an issue. Our biggest problem was that we were now off the books by a couple of miles, and we needed someone we could trust. And I knew just the right person, or persons to go to.

"I didn't think I would be hearing from you so soon," Cara said.

"We're in the top of the eighth, and it all depends on the next swing," I told her.

"You'd better tell me."

So I did.

"And you can't trust anyone?"

"No."

"Oh, dear, you are in a pickle," Cara said to me.

"I'd say it's a little worse, but that about covers it."

"Give me an hour and I'll talk to Miriam," Cara said.

An hour later, Cara got in contact. "I've done all I can, Reaper."

"What was the result?" I asked, expecting very little by her tone.

"I managed to pry a C-17 command platform loose as well as a UCAV along with a few other things. Miriam said if you break anything, you bought it."

"That sounds like the boss."

"She also said for you to watch your ass and don't go getting yourself killed. She still has a use for you."

"And that sounds more like her," I said. "Thanks, Cara."

I relayed the news to the others and we began to make a plan.

It was simple. Knocker and I would parachute from the command platform, with a Zodiac, come up on the ship, board it, and secure it as quietly as possible before securing the device.

Why weren't we taking more people? Because we didn't have any. And the fewer who knew about it the better off we were.

"What do we have, Slick?" I asked.

"Including the bridge," he said, "we have eight tangos topside. Below deck, there are another five."

I looked over a satellite photo, looking where he'd marked out roughly the positions of the lookouts. Knocker and I studied it for a moment before he said,

"Looks like we board on the starboard side, Reaper. We can start work from there."

I nodded. "I think you're right. If we get the Zodiac up alongside the ship and then board from there."

"What will you do with the Zodiac after that?" Holly asked.

"We will fix it to the side of the ship."

"That's just in case we need a quick getaway," Knocker said.

I said, "We'll secure the bow of the ship first and then work our way down the port side."

"I think we should secure that starboard lookout first," Knocker said. "From there, we can use all the containers to our advantage."

"Okay. Once the deck is secure, then we take the lookouts and the bridge."

He nodded. "Sounds good to me. There is one question I have though."

"What's that?"

He shook his head. "Doesn't matter. If it comes to that, we're fucked anyway."

"Love your optimism."

I looked over at Slick. "What is the weather like for tomorrow night?"

"No moon, but the weather's fine."

"Then that is when we go."

He looked at the map. "The ship should be somewhere off Malta by then."

"Good, we'll be able to have a holiday when we're done. You can all come back to my place."

With the plan set, we checked our equipment. Everything was in good working order. This wasn't our first ship interdiction. However, this wasn't as easy as the others were. Any number of things could go wrong. I wasn't the only one with concerns.

Holly came over to me after everyone had gone in their own direction. "Are you sure just the two of you can do this?"

I grinned. "I guess we'll find out."

"I'm serious. I can see if I can get you some backup."

I shook my head. "Too risky. If word gets out, who knows what will happen. Knocker and I can do this."

"I sure hope so, Reaper."

———

After parachuting from the plane, we'd climbed into the small dinghy and changed out of our wetsuits. When we were ready, we set out after the ship, the Zodiac skipping across the water of the Mediterranean as we approached the ship from astern. Knocker was driving and I was sitting up at the bow.

We'd decided that approaching from that direction to be our best option for going unnoticed. Once we were close enough, Knocker pulled out from behind it, the Zodiac bouncing over the wake before moving up beside the vessel.

Once we came alongside, he kept pace. I grabbed the telescopic boarding ladder and extended it full length before placing it over the side guardrail. Taking the long rope attached to the bow of the Zodiac, I started upward. Reaching the top, I made sure that no one was present before climbing over and securing the rope. This allowed Knocker to cut the engine and then commence his own ascent. A few minutes later, he joined me on the starboard side.

"Talk to me, Slick."

"Reaper, starboard. Tango is now approaching."

"Roger that."

Slipping into the shadowy shelter of a nearby container, we waited. At first, all we could hear was the low hum of the ship. After almost a minute, we heard a footfall then nothing for several seconds before another was heard. Beside me, I sensed Knocker on the move as he extracted his combat knife. A couple of heartbeats later, the tango appeared, and Knocker slipped out and intercepted the figure. Clamping his hand over the man's mouth, Knocker drove his knife deftly between ribs and into the man's heart.

Without letting go, he dragged the guard back into the shadows, wiping the knife on the man's clothing. Straightening up, Knocker slipped the knife back into its sheath and said, "One less for breakfast in the morning."

"Alpha, we're now moving toward the bow."

"Copy. Tango still in position, looks all clear."

Using the containers as cover, we moved carefully toward the bow of the ship. Drawing closer, we noticed the guard standing out in the open. There was no way of using a knife on him without being seen. I turned back and looked at Knocker, whispering, "Slick, where's that second bow guard?"

"He's still in position over your left shoulder."

I said to Knocker, "We'll take them both at once."

"Roger that. Just give me time to get in position."

He melted back into the shadows and I soon lost

sight of him. Then, moments later, I heard him say in my ear, "Bravo Two in position."

"On my mark."

My suppressed Heckler and Koch 416 came up. I sighted on the guard and then counted backward. "Three...two...one...execute."

Caressing the trigger on the 416, the recoil drove back into my shoulder. For good measure, I fired twice to make sure that he went down and stayed down. Once more in my ear, I heard a voice, "Tango down."

"Roger that."

Which left one guard on the port side. Knocker materialized out of the shadows and joined me, saying, "One more to go, and then we work the bridge."

Treading lightly across the steel decking, we kept to the shadows as much as possible until reaching the vicinity of the last guard. Drawing his knife once more, Knocker silenced him deftly, but instead of dragging the body back into the shadows, he sheathed his knife, then lifted the body and tipped it over the side.

"I hope he can swim."

Indicating the bridge with my hand, I said, "Let's get those two up top."

Remaining on high alert but knowing that Slick had our backs, we headed toward the bridge. Separating, we took up positions. Our weapons came up, sighting on both men who stood near the rail at the front of the bridge. "Tell me when you're ready."

"Let's party like you mean it."

"Three...two...one...execute."

Again, we each fired at the same time, and the two

tangoes on the bridge dropped. Now it was time to assault the wheelhouse. "Alpha, we need a sitrep."

"Everything looks fine, Bravo."

"Copy. Going up."

Entering through a hatch at the front of the bridge, we located the internal staircase and commenced a steady climb. Reaching the wheelhouse, Knocker opened the hatch.

The interior of the wheelhouse was illuminated by low-running lights. Taking a deep breath, I stepped through the doorway. On duty were two men: one was the first mate, the other was the helmsman. There was, however, an unexpected third person not previously detected. By then, it was almost too late.

Stepping from the shadows in the corner was a guard in a gray uniform, his weapon raised and about to shoot me in the back of the head. With a barely audible grunt, the man fell to the carpeted floor, a bullet hole in his head where Knocker punched his ticket. I glanced down at the lifeless body.

Knocker said, "Son of a bitch almost gave you another hole to talk out of."

"Remind me to buy you a beer."

Keeping my weapon trained on the first mate and the helmsman, I ordered, "Okay, step over here."

When they didn't respond, I changed to Russian. "Step over here now."

The pair moved toward me, their hands lifted in the universal gesture for surrender. Knocker stepped in behind them, pulled their hands down, and secured them behind their back.

I said, "Sit him down over there and let me talk to the first mate."

The helmsman was lowered to the floor against the bulkhead, his back pressed firmly against it. I stared at the first mate, asking him, "Where is the captain?"

"In his cabin."

"Where is the ship going?"

"Portsmouth."

"Shit." I glanced at Knocker. "As good a target as any I guess."

"Good thing we came when we did."

"Where is Igoshin?"

The man said nothing.

"Let's try this again. Where is Igoshin?"

"He is in the hold," the man replied.

"How many people?"

"What?"

I sighed. "How many people are with him?"

"Three."

"Is he guarding the package?"

The man nodded slowly.

"Do you know what the package is?" I asked.

He shook his head. "No, we were never told."

"Probably a good thing."

The man was curious. "What do you mean?"

"You are carrying a nuclear weapon," I told him.

"Oh, no." His face became a mask of fear.

"How many more of Igoshin's people are here?" I asked.

"Just those with him."

"Okay, sit down over there," I said to him.

"I want to help," the first mate said. "The crew has nothing to do with this. I will keep the ship running."

I stared at him doubtfully. "Why would you do that?"

"Like I said, the crew have nothing to do with this. Also, look out there."

He pointed at the water ahead of the bow. He said, "We have a course change coming up, and do you see those lights out there?"

"Yes."

"They are other ships. If we go out of our lane, we will crash into them."

"We could stop," I told him.

"Then Igoshin will know something is wrong," Knocker pointed out.

I studied the man in front of me, dubious of his motives. Every instinct screamed at me not to trust him, but there was something about his offer. I said, "You know, if we don't stop this nuke, you're as dead as us, right?"

"That is why I am helping you. No other reason."

I cut him free. "What about your helmsman?"

"He has as much to lose as I do."

Handing the first mate my knife, I said, "Cut him loose."

Presented with the perfect opportunity to kill me, I figured that if he was going to do it, this would be the time. Instead, he turned to his helmsman and cut the bonds. When the man got to his feet, there was a quick discussion, and then the helmsman returned to his post. The first mate, however, returned the knife to me and said, "You will need me to guide you to the hold. It will be quicker that way."

"Fine, lead the way."

Heading below decks, we followed him down through some hatches. When we eventually reached the hold where Igoshin was hiding, he whispered, "They are in there."

I glanced at Knocker. There was no need for words. Grabbing a flashbang, he pulled the pin. Then we moved.

The sound of the stun grenade going off in the hold was deafening. I heard cries of alarm, but by that time, we were among them.

Two well-placed rounds from my 416 hammered into the chest of a man closest to me. He cried out in pain, then fell to the deck. Beside me, I heard Knocker's 416 rattle off a couple of shots and a second man died. Neither was Igoshin. That left two mercenaries. One of them had to be the leader.

There was no time to work out which. It was imperative that we put them down fast and hard. I neutralized the one on the left while Knocker shot the one on the right, rendering the hold secure. Only seconds had elapsed since we'd opened the door.

While checking the dead men over, it became evident that the mercenary leader wasn't among them. I cursed under my breath and walked out of the hold and found the first mate still standing there in shock at the violence he'd been witness to.

I grabbed his shirt, "Come with me."

We entered the hold to find Knocker standing over one of the dead men. He looked up at me and said, "I double-checked them, Reaper. He's not here."

I turned to the first mate and said, "You told us that Igoshin was here."

He nodded vigorously. "That's right, he is."

"You look at all four of these bodies and tell us which one."

Tentatively, the first mate stepped forward. He looked at the first two bodies and shook his head. When he got to the third, he pointed and said, "That is him."

I shook my head. "That's not him."

Knocker reached into his pocket and withdrew his cell. He took a photo of the dead man's face and relayed it back to the platform overhead. "Alpha, I'm sending you a picture. I need an identification. Our HVT is not here. I say again, our HVT is not on board."

My next thought was that perhaps the nuke wasn't here either. Then, Knocker said, "Do you hear that?"

I listened intently. At first, I could only hear the steady thrum of the ship's engines. Then, after a moment, I picked up the small beep, beep, beep. My body tensed as concern washed over me. "It can't be."

"You have got to be fucking kidding me," Knocker growled.

"Find it," I snapped.

It didn't take us long. We only needed to follow the sound, which led us to a large crate. It was sealed tight. "We need to get it open."

Knocker looked at the first mate. "Do you have anything we can open it with?"

"Yes, I think so."

He disappeared, and my friend shook his head. "Take your time, we've got it. Take all the time in the world. We're just going to die, that's all."

He reappeared moments later. In his hand was a small pry bar. He handed it over, and I immediately forced it into the small gap beneath the lid and started to lever it up. The nails gave way with a piercing shriek, and soon, we had the lid off.

"Shiiit," Knocker said in a low voice.

Having located what we were looking for, we glanced down at the countdown clock. There was only one minute thirty left to do something about it.

"That's not good. They must have armed it when we came in."

"Digital timer, tamper proof mechanism, junction box, power source, tamper proof on that. I see eight wires and I'm guessing that if we cut any of them, it goes boom."

One minute.

"What do you suggest?"

"How flexible are you?" Knocker asked.

"What the fuck has that got to do with it?"

"Well, if you're flexible enough, you can kiss your ass goodbye."

"Great solution," I said.

Stepping back, I took out my Glock and raised it. Pointing it at the mechanics of the bomb, I saw Knocker's eyes widen. "What the fuck are you doing, you crazy pillock?"

"I'm going to shoot it."

Thirty seconds.

"You shoot that thing, and you'll kill us all."

"Hello, nuclear bomb. Do you have a suggestion?"

"Yeah, cut the fucking wire."

"Which ones, dickhead?"

"I don't know, take your pick."

Fifteen seconds.

I said, "We don't have time."

"Shit, cut the wire going to the power source," Knocker said.

Ten seconds.

"Do you have wire cutters?"

"Don't be stupid. Of course I don't."

"Fuck it," I growled and shot the bomb.

"You shot the bomb?" German asked, perplexed.

I nodded. "We didn't have time to do anything else."

"That was a stupid thing to do," Miriam Craig said.

"It would have been even stupider if the bomb had gone off, and we wouldn't be here to tell you about it," Knocker shot back at her.

"Just shut up," German said. "I want to know what happened."

Knocker looked straight at him. His face is deadpan. "Well, Mr. German, we died."

"What the hell happened?" I asked Knocker, opening one eye.

He still had both eyes closed. "I don't know."

I looked at the bomb. The counter was on zero. "Why didn't it go off?"

Finally, Knocker opened both eyes and leaned over the bomb. He laughed out loud.

"What is so funny?"

"It's bloody fake," Knocker informed me.

"Which means, genius, the real one's still out there."

He looked at me and said, "No, it means we're still alive."

CHAPTER 12

ONE MONTH LATER

Knocker had been right, unfortunately. The bomb had been fake. Which meant it was still out there somewhere and we had no idea where. And by some miracle, it hadn't been detonated. This begged the question, why not?

It turns out that Morozov had convinced Lash to wait. Although the Russian thrust had been curtailed, NATO troops continued to gather, their contingency should it start up once more.

Paris was where we had flown, figuring that it was as good a target as any. However, in the four-week period that we'd been in limbo, our attempts at gaining intel by running down a few leads had failed to produce anything. We were still empty-handed.

After having our ties severed with MI6, we found ourselves working for the Ministry of Defense. Don't ask me how it came about, it was too complex. Suffice it to say that Holly was responsible for the negotiations and most of the maneuvering. Our boss was a colonel by the name of Helen March. Slick was collaborating with their intelligence officers as they assessed the situation throughout Europe.

Of Igoshin and Morozov, there was no sign. It was always good to hear from Miriam Craig, who checked in with us occasionally to assure us we still had her support. For the time being.

Meanwhile, back in Moscow, troops had been withdrawn beyond the borders, but Lash was still rattling his saber. Boris Pushkin was working behind the scenes from his hiding place in England to garner support and undermine the current leadership.

Thirty-two days after securing the ship in the Med, we were called in for a briefing. The mission's goal was to retrieve a hard drive from a large private hotel in Barcelona owned by a man named Santiago Ruiz.

"What is so important about him?" I asked.

Slick was nervous. "Have you ever seen the John Wick movies?"

"Sure."

"That's what the hotel is like. The one in the movies is based on this."

"Why haven't I ever heard of it before?" I asked.

"No one talks about it because no one goes there. Not normal people. If they do, it's always booked out."

"And this is where the hard drive is kept?"

"Yes."

"Why do we need it?" I asked.

"Names and places of residence," Slick said. "It's like an address book for the killer elite."

"Still doesn't tell me why we need to go there. Except maybe to get killed."

"We're working on the assumption that the Thomis sisters have knowledge of where the bomb has gone. To find them, we need the hard drive."

"So we break in, steal the hard drive, and try to get out without getting killed," Knocker said with more than a hint of doubt.

"Yes," Holly said.

"You might as well just put the gun to my head and pull the fucking trigger now."

"I thought a challenge like this was right up your street," she said to Knocker, hoping to spark something in him.

"I've changed my mind. I'd rather stay alive."

"Okay. So if we have to do it, we have to do it," I said. "Is there no other way?"

"No, at this point, we can't find anyone else."

I nodded. "I love a good Hail Mary."

"Good, let's get it set up."

Holly and Slick departed, leaving me and Knocker to discuss the mission.

He said, "You know this is batshit crazy, right?"

"Without a fucking doubt."

The Ministry of Defense loved the idea. For the simple fact it gave them a chance to get their own hands on the highly prized intelligence on the hard drive. There was no telling how they could use it. The information they might gain from it could be passed on to MI5 or MI6.

However, to gain access, we were going to need disguises. This was one job we couldn't carry out under our own identities. For once, word got out there'd be killers hunting us across the globe. And that was something we couldn't afford. Eventually they'd get lucky and take us off the board.

The MOD's SFX people had been brought in to work with us, flying to Barcelona, where we set up in a safehouse at the edge of the city. There were the four of us, the two special effects people, and three guys with no names who would watch over things for the duration of the op.

We planned to go that evening. Slick had supplied us with legends that were fully backstopped. There were also addresses to feed into the database. The plan was to check into a room, and then once we were prepared, Slick would put the security feed on a loop, and we'd go to work.

"You need to go to the second floor, right-wing," he told us. "There is a large room there housing multiple servers. That's where you need to be. I'll guide you through it once you gain access. Just remember, you're in a place where everyone could and would kill you."

"How is our extract coming?" I asked Holly.

"Once you get to the roof, it'll be waiting."

The roof had been chosen because of ease of access on both sides, and for it being the most expedient for a rapid exfil should anything happen. It was large enough and flat enough to land an MH-6 Little Bird.

Spending the next couple of hours resting, we then began our metamorphosis. It would take six hours for the transformation to be completed.

When the SFX people were done, the pair of us

were unrecognizable. I had a goatee beard, freckles, and red hair, my tattoos concealed. Knocker also wore a goatee beard, had blond hair, blue eyes, glasses, and was dressed in a suit. His tattoos were also covered.

And that was the easy part. All we had to do now was get in.

————

The magnificent four-story hotel was of sandstone construction and covered most of the block on which it stood in Barcelona's heart. Walking confidently up the steps, Knocker and I entered through the front door and were greeted by an enormous lobby complete with marble floor tiles. There were numerous artworks on the wall, and dark stained timber. On either side of us, placed at twenty-foot intervals, were concrete plinths holding busts of someone famous. We were ushered toward the main reception desk by these nameless faces.

The man in attendance at the counter was impeccably dressed in a dark suit with a bow tie. He looked at us both over the top of his glasses and said, "How may I help you today, sirs?"

"We would like a room," I said.

"I'm sorry, we are booked out."

I reached into my pocket and took out a replica of a star medallion. I sat it on the desk and the man glanced at it before looking up at me again.

"Have you stayed with us before, sir?"

"No."

"Name, please, sir?"

"Simon Oliver."

He looked at Knocker. "And yours, sir?"

"John Grayson."

"Just one moment."

He activated a touch screen computer inlaid into the countertop, his fingers dancing across it deftly. After a minute had elapsed, he looked back up and said, "Passports, please, sirs."

Reaching inside our coat pockets we retrieved the fake passports, sliding them across the counter to the man who took them. He then opened both and turned them face down on top of the screen so they could be scanned.

With that done, he closed them again and handed them back to us. Then he waited. "It shouldn't be a moment, sir."

I stood and nonchalantly gazed around the reception area. People were scattered throughout, some standing talking, others perusing newspapers while sitting on the lounges. It was just like in the movies.

On the far wall was a set of double wooden doors. I looked at the man behind the counter and I asked, "What's through there?"

"That would be the restaurant, sir. Will you be dining in your room tonight or in the restaurant, sir?"

Fuck it. "I think we'll dine in the restaurant."

"Good choice, sir." He was about to say something else when he looked back at his screen. "All seems to be in order, sir."

"Great."

"Will you be staying with us long?"

I nodded. "A couple of nights until our business is complete."

"Is there anything that you might require?"

"No, I think we're right." I looked at Knocker. "Anything you require?"

"No, I'm good, old chap."

I looked back at the reception manager. "Thank you, but I do believe we are fine."

He turned away to retrieve a keycard then brought it to his screen and programmed it, handing it over to me. It was red and resembled an ATM or credit card. "Room 302, sir. Take the elevator to the third floor, turn to your left, then it's the second door on your right. Enjoy your stay with us."

We retrieved our luggage and began walking toward the bank of elevators. I pressed the call button, and we waited for the car to arrive. When the chime sounded softly, the doors opened, and we stepped into the carpeted vestibule. I pressed the #3 button to take us to that floor. The doors were sliding closed when I heard, "Hold the elevator."

I stuck my hand out, sending the doors retracting once more. A woman, her lithe body clad in a tight red mini dress, stepped into the car, her red high heels accentuating shapely calves. She smiled at me, exposing straight white teeth. "Thank you."

Her accent was British. Leaning across me, she pressed the elevator button for the fourth floor. She straightened back up. Knocker was standing behind her, and I knew his eyes were burning into her tight buttocks. She knew it too, because her handbag suddenly fell to the elevator floor. Bending from the waist, keeping her legs straight, she bent over to pick it up, causing the dress to ride tantalizingly up her thighs. It stopped just before exposing the flesh of her buttocks, then she straightened slowly, adjusting the stretchy red fabric.

I rolled my eyes.

The elevator stopped on three, and the door slid open. We stepped out into the hallway, the patterned maroon carpet running the whole length. Before the doors could close on the elevator again, the woman called after us, "I'll be in the dining room at 7:00 if you'd care to join me."

When we reached our door, I tapped the keycard and the lock clicked audibly. I pushed it open, and we took our bags inside, Knocker closing and locking the door behind us. With that, I turned on my friend. "What the hell were you doing?"

"Enjoying the view?"

"You know she knew you were enjoying the view, don't you?"

"Of course I do, that's why she did it. Don't forget we have a date at 7:00."

"Son of a bitch. That's all we need."

Knocker stared at me. "You know there's something not right about her, don't you?"

"No shit, Dick Tracy. And we need to find out what it is before we do anything tonight."

"Flash room, Reaper."

It was a spacious suite with tasteful décor and muted wallpaper. Both bedrooms had their own en suite and a king-size four-poster bed. Wall sconces appeared to be the only lighting in the living area, making it dim but not dark. Then I realized why. Crossing to the light switch, I turned the knob and the lights came up. I reached into my pocket and retrieved a small container with two earwigs in it. I handed one to Knocker and put the other one in my ear. "Alpha, copy?"

"Read you, Lima Charlie, Bravo One."

"Eagle has landed. We're all good so far."

"Copy that."

"Just so you're aware, there may be a fly in the ointment. We'll know more later."

"What do you mean by a fly, Bravo?" Holly asked, joining the conversation.

"A female fly. She's British, not bad looking, but there's something about her."

"Roger that. Keep me updated."

———————

When seven p.m. arrived, we were already on our way down to the restaurant. We were shown to a table beside a large plate glass window with views out onto the street. Sitting down, we began perusing the menu. The vibe we were getting was one of suspicion. But I guess in a place like this, suspicion was to be expected.

"Mind if I join you?"

Looking up, we saw the woman from the elevator. Gone was the red dress, a short black one with a plunging neckline in its place. A necklace tattoo disappeared into her cleavage. Her lipstick was almost mahogany.

"Take a seat," I replied, and she pulled out the chair opposite me. "I'm Simon Oliver."

She looked at Knocker. "Who might this chocolate delight be?"

He shook his head. "Now I know she's taking the piss."

The woman feigned indignation. "Me? Taking the piss?"

I stared at her. "Six?"

"Five."

"Christ, what are you doing here?" Knocker asked.

"What are you doing here? What banner are you flying under?"

In my ear, Slick said to me, "Reaper, code red."

I stared at her for a moment and said, "Mario Ricci."

Mario Ricci was a backstop. Should it be investigated, they would come up with him as being one of the biggest organized crime bosses in Italy. Further digging would show he was under investigation by Interpol as well as several intelligence agencies.

"Good save," said Slick. "She is Maryanne Fleetwood. Head of hotel security."

I showed no sign I'd heard what he'd just told me. Neither did Knocker. The woman raised her eyebrows. "Mario Ricci? What business does he have in this modest city?"

"The quiet kind," I replied.

She gave me a coy smile. "How about we skip dinner and go back to my suite?"

"What about my friend?"

"He can join us too."

A broad grin split my face. "As wonderful as that sounds, I think we should probably decline."

Raising an eyebrow at me, she said, "That's too bad." Then she got to her feet and said, "Maybe I'll catch you around."

As she walked away, Knocker opened his mouth to speak. I quickly put a finger to my lips to cut him off. He frowned as I got up and moved around to where the woman had been seated. Sliding my hand beneath the table, my fingers felt around until I found it. When my hand came out, it was holding a small microphone.

My next movement was to discreetly throw it under a table further down the row from where we sat. "Good save by Slick," Knocker said.

"Yes."

We ordered our meals and once they arrived, we consumed them while Slick was updating us on the layout. "It looks like security roams throughout the hotel. The server room has three guards. All of whom are linked into the main security room which has four people controlling the show with Maryanne Fleetwood overseeing them."

"Who is she, anyway?" I asked before shoveling food into my mouth with a heavy silver fork.

"Former British army colonel who worked for military intelligence black ops. She had her own team. Something went wrong in Greece, and she quit. With a woman of her talent, she had any number of suitors. This is where she landed."

When our plates were empty, we headed back toward our suite. On our way, we saw one of the guards. He was armed with an MP5.

"Slick, are you still there?" Knocker asked.

"Roger?"

"Say something happens and the police are called. What's the go?"

"There is usually a certain amount of money which changes hands, and they keep it in-house."

Having made it safely to our suite, we gathered our weapons and waited. When it came to operations such as this, things had a way of going terribly wrong. Maybe this one would be different.

CHAPTER 13

Yeah, I was wrong.

Slapping home a magazine on the MP5 I'd taken from a dead guard, I opened fire as bullets hammered into the servers all around me. I looked over at Knocker and shouted, "Will you hurry the fuck up."

"These things take time, Simon old son."

I was amazed that he could actually remain in character under the circumstances.

How did we get here? Let me explain.

When it was time to move, we left our room. Slick had already placed the security camera feed on a loop, which we hoped would fool anyone in the security center long enough for us to get our work done.

We planned to use the stairwell to skirt the roving patrols and move to level two. However, that hotel at night was unlike anything we had ever encountered before. Our first inclination was witnessing a couple having sex in the hallway. The guy had her pressed against the wall while building up a full head of steam. Then, as we walked past another doorway, screams of pain emanating from within gave Knocker and I pause, and we were about to move on when the door opened wide enough for us to see past the person filling the void.

As we looked beyond the man's shoulder, we saw a woman wearing nothing but a plastic apron, blood dripping from it, while she worked with a Sawzall on some poor soul fixed to a rack.

"What fuck you look at," the man snarled in halting English.

The woman spotted us and gave us a finger-wiggling wave. Suddenly, I realized who it was. Maryanne Fleetwood. She'd obviously gone completely to the dark side and was inflicting an unbelievable amount of pain on the poor bastard she was working on.

"Sick bitch," Knocker said under his breath.

She walked toward the doorway after placing the Sawzall on a small table next to some other tools of her trade. "Hi, boys."

There were flecks of blood on her face and her exposed skin. "Care to come in? I'm about to get to the good part. I'm going to remove his balls the old-fashioned way. Open the sack and use the teeth to extract them."

"Poor cunt," Knocker said solemnly.

"What did he do?" I asked.

"He broke one of the rules," she replied.

"Just one?"

"Yes, just one. So, will you join me?"

"No, I think we'll pass."

"Pity, I get really worked up doing this, and once I've finished, I do love a hot shower."

"Yeah, enjoy it."

The door closed and she went back to her task. So did we. However, she'd already made us. I don't know how, but she had.

Further along the hallway near the bank of elevators, we were passed by a Chinese man with a black woman on either arm. Both women wore strings of diamonds around their throats, linked together with piano wire.

How did he know that, I hear you ask. Because I knew the women. You might think them African by the color of their skin, but they were West Indian. They were the Jackson sisters. Dolly and Rose. Voodoo worshippers and more than capable assassins. The guy between them, I guessed, was their next victim.

Earlier, I mentioned the movie John Wick. In the hotel in that movie, there was to be no killing. Here, they just cleaned up after their guests.

But that doesn't explain how I actually knew them. A little while back, I had been in Jamaica looking for a priest who had been into live sacrifices. MI6 had sent me there to take him out. However, the priest had a couple of nuns in his employ. They just happened to be the Jackson sisters.

I'd prepped for the kill, scouted the streets, and worked all the possible problems I might encounter. The local MI6 officer in charge on the ground showed me their handiwork. It was a photo of a man with his tongue removed and his chest cavity opened so the heart could be extracted.

My final decision on the kill was to use a rifle from a church tower as he emerged from his home. They were with him, one on either side. When I stroked the trigger, the rifle slammed back into my shoulder and the bullet flew true. The voodoo man died. "Someone is getting unlucky tonight," Slick said over the comms.

"You know them?" I asked.

"The Jacksons, sure. They've come across my screen before. Just like the two about to get out of the second elevator."

"Who might that be?"

"The Baron and Wilhelmina."

"You are fucking kidding me," Knocker said.

When the elevator doors slid open, a middle-aged man wearing a suit stepped out with a woman attired in a long green gown. Baron von Brauchitsch and Wilhelmina descended from German aristocracy.

They were the Assassin Lovers. Their relationship was legendary. The Baron used her as his honey trap. She'd lure the target in, and he'd kill them. Simple, but effective.

They walked past us, and I caught the heavy scent of her perfume. My guess was that they were just returning from a job.

Knocker said, "I'm starting to wish I had me a big bomb, Simon."

I nodded. "I agree, John."

"Bravo, the stairwell is clear."

"Roger," I whispered.

Opening the door into the stairwell we started down, the rubber soles of our shoes keeping the noise to a minimum, helping us reach the landing in almost total silence. On the door leading into the second floor was a large sign that said *KEEP OUT* and *STAFF ONLY*.

That didn't apply to us because we were neither

staff nor could we read. So, we went in. What we found beyond the door was quite astounding. Bank after bank of servers drawing an inordinate amount of power. There was no sign of any guards.

Behind us, Knocker closed the door quietly. I whispered into my comms, "I have no vision inside, Bravo. From here out, you're on your own."

"At least tell me what the fuck I'm looking for."

"You're looking for a screw-on panel. When you remove that, you'll see a long blue cable. That'll lead you to the hard drive."

"What fucking panel, Slick? There are—"

"Hey!"

I turned and looked at the guard who'd discovered us. "Fuck it."

Knocker's suppressed Glock came out and he shot the man twice in the chest. There was no other way around it.

During his fall, the guard squeezed the trigger of his MP5, the bullets spraying the closest server.

"That's just bloody wonderful," Knocker said as he hurried over to the fallen man.

He bent down and picked up the MP5. Then grabbed spare magazines. "Here," he said and tossed them to me. "You can use that."

"What are you going to do?" I asked.

"Find a bloody needle in a haystack." He grinned at me. "Slick, tell me where to find that fucking thing or I'll tell your new girlfriend you slept with her sister."

"How do you know she has one?"

"How do you know she doesn't?"

"You're an asshole."

"Yeah, but I'm useful."

"Most assholes are."

Sudden gunfire shredded the air around us as the second of the three guards found us. I ducked back behind a server bank while Knocker scrambled for cover. Bullets hammered into the server and electrical sparks showered the floor.

"I sure hope that drive wasn't in there."

Through our comms, I could hear Knocker encouraging Slick in his usual style. Slick, on the other hand, was giving as good as he got. Myself, I was still trying to kill the second server room guard while knowing that the third was out there somewhere.

More bullets came my way, hammering into the thin sides of the server. It sounded like a hailstorm on a tin roof. I leaned around and fired. The MP5 rattled off a long burst and the magazine went dry.

I began to reload.

Yes, this is where I started.

I looked around and saw Knocker. "Will you hurry the fuck up?"

"A man can only work as fast as his hired help. In this case, the bloody pillock is a turtle."

"Screw you."

"Slick, it's not this one."

"Then try another. It will have—"

Another burst of gunfire drowned out his transmission. In a way, I was glad it was Knocker and not me. Once more, I fired around the corner. This time, I was lucky enough to hit some exposed leg. It was some use. For the appendage buckled and the guard fell out from cover. Then I had a better shot, and he died.

The third guard, however, had decided that

flanking me was a good option, and I only caught his movement to my right before he fired.

Throwing myself to the floor, I rolled as bullets chased me, searching for flesh. Coming up once more, I fired, forcing him back into cover. I leaped back behind a different server bank, my shoulder crashing into it, hard.

"Bravo, there might be a new problem."

"Such as?" I asked.

"It looks like your friend is arming the natives from the hotel armory."

"The hotel has an armory?" I asked.

"Big one, by the looks of it."

"Shit. John, find it or forget it. We're running out of time." My last words were almost drowned out by a fresh blast of gunfire.

Gathering myself, I fired a long burst before crossing the space to change the angle. When the guard fired again, he had no idea I was no longer there, and bullets hammered opposite. The next time, I was waiting for him, and once exposed, bullets from my MP5 ripped into his body.

"That's all three down, where are we at?"

"I found it, but am just getting it out."

"Hurry up." I had an idea. "Slick, are the cameras still on loop?"

"Affirmative."

"Okay."

"Knocker, you got it?"

"Yeah."

"Okay, let's go. Leave your gun hidden."

"What?"

"They still don't know who we are. We go charging

around with MP5s, we're in trouble. Slick, get that helicopter in here."

"On its way."

I threw the MP5 down and we hurried toward the door. "Slick, what is the stairwell like?"

"If you go up now, you should be fine."

Doing as he suggested, we began moving up the stairs, and as we reached three, Slick said, "You've got a couple of guards coming down."

There was nowhere to go. We braced ourselves and expected the worst.

As soon as they saw us, the first security guard shouted at us in Spanish, "Get out of the way!"

Pressing ourselves against the wall, they pushed past and continued to descend. Heading up once more, we soon reached the rooftop, the sound of the incoming helicopter audible through the door. There was, however, one more obstacle. They had a security guard on the roof. He was standing in the middle of the rooftop, waving at the helicopter.

Due to the noise of the helicopter, he didn't hear us coming, and I took advantage, rushing up behind him and hitting him over the head with my Glock. He dropped like a stone, and I pulled him out of the landing zone. Moments later, the helicopter landed, and we climbed aboard.

That had gone a lot better than I had feared it would. I looked over at Knocker as the helicopter rose into the air. "Good show, John."

"Very good show, Simon."

————————

Two hours later, we were back in the safehouse, and Slick was analyzing the data. "This is amazing," he said. "It's a real who's who of the killer elite."

"There are only two killer elite that we need to find, Slick," I told him.

"Yes, and I've got them in Cagliari, Sardinia."

"That's good."

"Yes and no. When Knocker ripped it out—"

"In my defense, I was in a hurry. We were getting shot at."

"When he ripped it out there was some corruption to the hard drive. I know the city but not the exact address. But that isn't the only reason."

"Why?"

"Cagliari is no longer the tourist mecca it used to be. It now is under the control of Carlo Bellini."

"The whole place?"

"Remember how it used to be a good place to go to get kidnapped for ransom?" Slick asked. "Bellini came in and organized it all. However, the tourist trade dropped away and he had to diversify his methods of doing business."

"Such as?" Knocker asked.

"He's taken kidnapping to the waters. His people intercept boats and work it that way."

"So he's a mafia pirate?" I asked.

"Basically."

"You say tourism has dropped off, but I'm guessing some still go there."

Slick nodded. "Yes, against government advice."

I looked over at Holly. "I guess me and the brutish one are going on holiday."

"Just don't get yourselves killed."

CHAPTER 14

It was easy to see why Sardinia had once been a destination for tourists. History had played its part in Cagliari's creation. Phoenicians, Carthaginians, Romans, and Byzantines all had their hand in the creative oven, and this was the result.

Knocker and I were in one of the historic districts, walking its narrow, winding streets lined with medieval architectural buildings.

We were looking for a café where we were to meet with Bruno Cameroni, known in the city as the machinegun lawyer. He'd gone to war with the mafia in the heyday of organized crime and been the last one standing—with the help of Carlo Bellini. Now he and Bellini had an understanding. It was simple. They left each other alone.

That didn't go for us though. Cameroni made sure we understood that. We were fair game if they chose to act.

Locating the café, we went inside. The waiter showed us to a table toward the rear and we sat down, a young waitress following with a carafe of coffee and two cups. It was strong and bitter and tasted good. I placed the cup back on the saucer and nodded. "Not bad."

"Better than that stuff you usually make," Knocker said.

We were both armed with Glocks. Mine was on my lap, out of sight. I guessed Knocker's was too. The waitress came back with the coffee pot. "Would you like a top-up?"

"Sure, thank you."

"You are tourist?" she asked.

"In a way," I replied. "Here to see an old friend."

"Really? Maybe I know them."

"Maybe," I said and left it at that.

After topping off both our cups, she walked away once more. I watched her for a time, noticing that she went to the telephone and made a call, speaking briefly before hanging up. Which was curious.

"Knocker, head on a swivel. We might have something coming down the pike."

"You know, one day, we might go somewhere to relax. You ever want to do that?"

"I have somewhere," I pointed out.

"Then maybe I might. I could move in beside you."

"The day you move in is the day my for-sale sign goes up," I replied.

"Some friend you are."

I caught movement at the door and watched an older man enter. He took off the hat he was wearing, revealing gray hair. He glanced at the waitress and nodded. She acknowledged him with a nod and looked over at our table, directing him with her dark eyes.

The man headed our way. As he did, I tightened my grip on the Glock. He stopped in front of our table. "Which one of you is Kane?"

"I am," I said.

"I am Bruno Cameroni."

"Take a seat." I indicated with my free hand to the chair opposite me, and he pulled it out and sat down. I said, "This is my friend Ray."

He ignored Knocker. "What is it you want from me?"

"Information," I said.

Starting to rise, he said, "Then you have come to the wrong place."

"It's important."

"When I was told you wanted to meet me, I wasn't informed what it was for. Now I know, I cannot help."

"We're looking for a nuclear weapon big enough to wipe out a small country."

"I don't know anything about such a thing," he replied brusquely.

"Yes, but you know someone who does," Knocker replied.

"Oh, yes?"

"Sonia and Louisa Thomis."

Cameroni sat down at the table. He stared hard at me before saying, "You obviously haven't heard."

"Heard what?" I asked.

"Sonia Thomis is dead."

This took me by surprise. "What happened to her?"

"I do not know," Cameroni said.

"Where will I find her sister?"

"They had an apartment inside the city."

I nodded. "Is there much security?"

Cameroni shrugged. "I'm sure a man with all your skills will be able to get past it."

"What about Carlo Bellini? Are we going to have trouble with him?"

Again, the shrug came. "I cannot tell you. But if you do, you must be prepared to fight. Carlo will not let you leave if he sets his mind to it."

"Then I guess we'd better be prepared, just in case. Now, where can we find Louisa Thomis?"

————

Using the directions supplied by Cameroni, we found the apartment near the center of one of the historical areas. It was quiet, early morning, just after two. Knocker picked the door lock, and we slipped inside.

And found Louisa waiting for us. She was seated in a chair, a glass of gin in one hand and a Beretta in the other. She was wearing a black dress, and in the orange lamp-light, she appeared to be sad. Down-trodden even.

She said, "I have been waiting for you. What took you so long?"

"We would have been here sooner, but we were given the wrong address," Knocker replied.

"You are here now."

"We heard about your sister."

"That was down to you."

"So what happens next?" I asked her. "Revenge?"

"I said it was down to you. I didn't say it was you.

No, my revenge is not against you. But you will help me."

"Okay, we're listening."

Louisa placed the drink on a small table and picked up a pack of cigarettes. She took one out and lit it. "My sister was killed by the people who hired us."

"Morozov and Igoshin?"

"Yes. They killed her because we allowed you to escape. I wish they had killed us both, but I knew you would come."

"So, if you don't want to kill us, what is it you're waiting for?"

Louisa said, "You have come here for information. Yes?"

"That's right," I replied.

"I will give you what I know. In return, you must promise to kill them for what they did."

I nodded. "Seems like a fair enough deal."

"We are not done yet," she said.

Knocker groaned. "Why do I get the feeling that we aren't going to like this?"

Louisa stared at him. "Do you want the information or not?"

"What else?" I asked, bringing her focus back to me.

"I want you to rescue Maryanne Fleetwood."

"That psycho bitch?" Knocker growled.

"That psycho bitch just happens to be the woman that I love," Louisa hissed.

"Where is she?" I asked resignedly.

"Don't tell me you're contemplating this, Reaper?" Knocker sounded perplexed.

"It might be the only way we find the nuke," I

replied. I stared at Louisa, my eyes becoming slits. "Do you know where it is?"

"Yes."

"If you're fucking with us, I'll let him cut your heart out along with your girlfriend's."

"You bring her to me and I will tell you what you want to know."

"Reaper, let's just torture it out of her."

I stared into her eyes but saw nothing. I said, "It won't work. We need to do this. Where is she?"

"Volturno Island off the coast of Spain. It is owned by Santiago Ruiz. He—"

"We know who he is," I replied, cutting her explanation off.

"There is an old fortress on the island. She is being held there."

"Why hasn't he killed her? More to the point, why is she locked up in the first place?"

"Because she is being held responsible for what happened at the hotel a month ago. Keeping her incarcerated is her punishment. God only knows what they are doing to her."

"Why haven't you gone after her yourself?" I asked.

"Because I am too close to the problem. And I knew you would come. I just didn't expect you to take this long."

"Okay, we'll do it. But we're going to need some things. Can you do that?"

"Yes. One thing I'm not short of is assets."

"There is one thing I won't guarantee," I cautioned her. "That's her safety. People sometimes pick up stray bullets."

"Just bring her to me. I need her."

"We'll be in touch."

———

"I don't bloody like it," Knocker growled once we were back on the street. "We're helping an assassin free her batshit crazy girlfriend from an island controlled by a psychopath, possibly guarded by an unknown quantity of killers. Have I missed anything out?"

"We need that information," I told him, ignoring his last question.

"We need to go back in there and torture it out of her before millions die."

"She won't give it up," I told him. "I saw it in her eyes."

"Let me cut the fuckers out and you'll see bloody pits."

"Come on, let's get out of here."

"*Might I ask why you would consider doing it?*" Miriam asked.

"*Because it was the only way to find out where the bomb was.*"

"*But you were dealing with a killer. One who was asking you to help an extremely sick individual escape from another killer.*"

"*It was the shortest route home.*"

"*We've heard a lot of questionable calls throughout this debrief, Mr. Kane,*" German said. "*This one just might be right up there.*"

I yawned. "*Can we just get on with this? This is the last*

day, and quite frankly, I've had enough. The sooner we get done, the better."

German nodded. "Continue."

I stabbed my finger at the map of the island. "We insert here and make our way to the old fortress. It is reasonably close to the target in the event that we have to carry her out."

"Okay. Are we swimming in?"

"Can't. Need to take a Zodiac."

"Fair enough."

"There will be no overwatch, no air support, anything like that," Holly informed us. "The MOD won't sanction any such thing for an op like this."

"Understood," I replied. "Which is why we're getting equipment from Louisa."

"You'll be on your own."

"Not like we've not been there before," I replied.

"Once you're done, head back to the mainland and we'll be there to help. Until then, we're just onlookers."

————

So, that's the way it happened. We took the Zodiac from the mainland and came up on a clean beach in the middle of the night. We pulled the small craft up the shore and checked our equipment. Putting masks on, we began moving toward the target.

Behind the beach was a layer of thick coastal brush. Carrying suppressed Heckler and Koch 433s, Knocker and I broke through the dense vegetation to see the fortress beyond.

Crouching at the edge of the brush line, we scanned the area through our NVGs, picking out two guards atop the walls, walking back and forth like sentries of old.

I tapped Knocker on the shoulder when I was sure there weren't anymore. We brought our weapons up simultaneously, and after a short pause, I said, "Send it."

Both weapons discharged and the two sentries disappeared below the parapets. Knocker and I hurried forward, stopping at the base of the wall. Waiting there, we listened for any sign of life. Certain that no one else was there, we fired our grappling hooks over the wall. I tugged on mine to make sure it was secure. When it didn't come back down at me, I took that as a good sign. Next, I hooked up my motorized ascender and started up. Knocker was close behind.

Climbing atop the battlements, we looked around after flipping our NVGs up. Beyond the pitted sandstone walls was a different world. Green lawns, manicured gardens, gravel drive covered in white stone. All around were decorative lawn lights. It was like a scene out of a James Bond movie.

We could only see three additional guards walking the grounds. There was no telling how many more were on site but not visible. I walked along the battlements until I reached some stone stairs that led down the inside of the wall. Knocker followed my lead and we descended silently.

At the bottom of the stairs, we crept into a lush garden. The trees and shrubs were tall enough to conceal us from the approaching guard. Knocker handed me his weapon while drawing his knife from its sheath.

As the guard drew adjacent to our position, Knocker slipped silently out of the darkness and clamped a hand over the guard's mouth while inserting the knife between his ribs. The sharp point found the man's heart and ended his life.

In a smooth and practiced movement, Knocker dragged him back into the garden to hide the body.

The second guard was taken out with a suppressed shot before his corpse was dragged into the shadows. The third one met a similar fate.

Knocker and I crouched against a wall of the main building. Like the outer walls, it was constructed of sandstone. He asked, "Where to?"

"Old places like this will have dungeons beneath it. I'm guessing we should go down."

When we slipped inside, we were immediately assailed by the old smell of the place. The floors were slate, and the walls sandstone like the exterior. All had some form of decoration to them.

We'd let our carbines fall and were now using our suppressed Glocks. If we were going to be discovered, this was when it would happen.

On cue, a man appeared ahead of us. He walked across the hallway, my Glock tracking him. By some miracle, he failed to look in our direction, and I held my fire. We crept forward cautiously. As we neared the room that the man had entered, we could hear voices.

I paused and listened. They were speaking about their prisoner and the fact that she wouldn't live for much longer. I felt myself growing concerned. If we failed to get Maryanne back, maybe Louisa would renege on providing us the intel we needed.

Using hand signals, I indicated to Knocker I was about to breach the room. I moved smoothly. "You lot should be in bed."

The man I'd seen in the hallway went for his weapon. I put a bullet in his chest and one in his head. By this time, Knocker was already in the room and covering the second man. I turned to him and said, "I assume you're Santiago Ruiz."

"Who are you?"

"Yeah, you don't need to know that," I replied.

"What do you want? You have no idea what you are doing."

"Take us to Maryanne," I said, ignoring him.

"No."

"Take us or I'll just shoot you and find her anyway," I said.

Ruiz rose from his seat and grunted. "Follow me."

Leading us to a door farther along the hallway he opened it. We found ourselves standing at the top of some stairs. The lights were on, so we didn't need to search for a switch. We followed him down into what used to be the fortress's dungeon. It was cold and damp.

He took us past the cells to a chamber. It could only be described as a chamber of horrors. And there on some kind of medieval torture rack was Maryanne: bloody and naked and dying.

I shook my head. "Knocker."

Without the need for additional words, Knocker

shot Ruiz in the head. My friend looked down at the body and said, "That was too good for him."

I checked Maryanne. She had been systematically tortured and was on the brink of the abyss. Her eyes fluttered open and she gave Knocker a weak smile. "The devil has come for me."

"Not the devil, lass, just someone sent by a friend."

"It is you. I know that voice."

"Yeah, it's me."

"Are you looking at—at my ass?"

He glanced at me before saying. "Yeah, it's perfect."

"Liar."

I said, "Louisa sent us to get you out."

Maryanne coughed weakly. "Too late. I'm dying."

My nod was sympathetic. No one deserved to die this way. I'm no angel, but I've never killed anyone like this. "You are."

"Do me a favor?"

"What?"

"Shoot me."

"Okay."

"I want to do something first," Maryanne said weakly.

"What?" I asked, grateful for the reprieve.

She related her desire to me, and for the next couple of minutes, we carried them out. By the time she was finished, she was even weaker. Maryanne closed her eyes and let out a small sigh. "I'm ready."

Then I shot her.

Preparing to leave, we took one last look at her broken body. Yes, we left her there. What else could we do? Retracing our steps, we made it to the exterior of the fortress, encountering no more problems. Ruiz was dead, so was Maryanne. All we had to do now was break the news to Louisa.

"She is dead, isn't she." It was a statement, not a question.

"We did what we could, but she was too far gone," I informed her. I took out my cell. "Here, press play."

Louisa looked askance at me before taking it. Knocker and I walked away while she watched Maryanne's final message. When she was done, we rejoined her. She looked up at us, tears in her eyes. "Thank you."

"There was nothing we could do."

"Ruiz?"

"He's dead," I replied.

"Then you did something."

"Yes."

Louisa paused and then said, "Michel was paid to transport the package and its escort to Brussels."

"What escort?"

"Grigori Igoshin and some handpicked people. Then Michel was told to run the second ghost train."

"The second?" Knocker asked.

"Yes. The weapon was on the first one we boarded. It was all a part of the ruse."

"Bollocks."

"But Igoshin didn't trust Fontaine?" I asked.

"He wasn't sure, so we were paid to make sure nothing happened."

"And we know what happened after that."

Louisa said nothing.

"And as far as you know, it's still there?" I asked.

She shook her head. "No, it has been moved again."

"Be fucked," Knocker growled. "We did all that for nothing."

"It gives you a place to start," she replied. "And a name."

"What name?" I asked. I too was getting irritated.

"Jan Witsel. He is another like Fontaine: a transporter," Louisa explained.

"Are you saying that he was the one who moved it?" I asked.

"It would make sense."

I could hear Knocker muttering under his breath. Then I asked Louisa, "Where in Brussels?"

"I don't know. He moves around. Now, I'd like to be left alone."

Nodding, I turned away. "Come on, Knocker. Let's go."

On the way out through the front door, we heard a loud gunshot.

———

Holly and Slick were waiting out front in a black SUV. I climbed in. Holly was behind the wheel. "Did you get that?"

"Slick is running him now."

"What about you?" I asked. "Have you heard of him before?"

"I think vaguely, but I can't be sure."

Knocker said, "I'm going to take a punt and say the target is good old Blighty. Like we already assumed."

"Good possibility."

"Got him," Slick said.

"Where?" I asked.

"Not got him, got him. I have information."

"All right, spill."

"Belgian native. Mother was a corporate highflyer, father a government man. Got to meet a lot of people. Even the bad ones, it seems. Daddy wound up in jail for selling secrets to the Germans. There was a big shitstorm over it. Looks like junior has taken over his father's illegalities."

"What happened to his mother?"

"She died. He inherited her fortune." Slick scrolled through the information. "He's on Interpol's watch list. He's been blamed for smuggling women, immigrants, weapons, and even uranium."

"Do any of you know anyone in Brussels who might be able to help out?"

Holly hesitated. I saw the look on her face.

"Holly?"

"I might know someone."

"Who?"

"Noah Smets. He's my uncle."

"Fine, let's look him up," Knocker suggested.

"It's not that easy," she replied.

"Why not?" I asked.

"Because he's otherwise engaged," she replied.

From the backseat, Slick said, "He's in prison."

"Yes."

"Why didn't this get flagged?" Christine Ryan asked.

"Because my father changed our name when we moved to London when I was a child," Holly said.

"But Holly isn't Belgian either?"

"My parents named me Hollandia. It was shortened when we moved."

"That isn't a common name in Belgium."

"My parents weren't common people."

Christine Ryan nodded and said, "Okay, I think we should take a break."

I said, "I thought—"

"A break, Mr. Kane."

"Yes, ma'am."

We filed out of the room and returned to the cafeteria. The woman behind the counter smiled wanly at me and said, "Still here."

"Last day," I replied.

Taking our seats at our usual table, Holly started to speak when I noticed Anesha enter the room. She started toward the counter after glancing in my direction. "Hold that thought," I said, getting to my feet.

I hurried through the tables to intercept her. She saw me coming and stopped. I said, "Congratulations on the promotion."

"Thank you, John."

"You never thought to mention it?"

"It had nothing to do with you."

Her point was blunt, and I felt as though I'd been slapped in the face. I nodded. "Fine."

Having been summarily dismissed, I turned to go back to the table.

"John, wait."

"You made yourself clear," I said over my shoulder. "I shouldn't have expected anything more."

I rejoined my colleagues at the table. Knocker said, "You want me to brush that layer of ice off you?"

"Just shut up." I took out my cell and dialed a number.

"Yes?"

"Bring him. Let me know when you get here."

"Roger that."

Twenty minutes later, we were back and running for the home plate.

CHAPTER 15

"LASH HAS JUST INFORMED THE WEST THAT HE HAS A nuke hidden on NATO soil and will use it if they don't accede to his demands," Slick told us. "He has given them three days to comply."

"What demands?" I asked.

"All NATO forces are to withdraw from Soviet territories to the border of Germany down to Bulgaria."

"They can't pull back everything in that time," Knocker pointed out.

"Lash has given them some leeway. If the forces are seen to be moving by then, he will give them another week. Failure to comply will result in detonation."

"That doesn't give us a lot of time."

"No, it doesn't," Holly said. "We can get into the prison this afternoon."

Having arrived in Brussels the night before, the MOD had put us up in a safe house within the city. Slick had been working tirelessly since, trying to find anything that might lead us to Jan Witsel. So far, he'd come up with nothing.

"This guy covers his tracks better than a fish in water," Slick said.

"Just do your best," I replied. "Maybe you'll get lucky."

"Yeah, who knows?"

I looked over at Holly. "Just what is it your uncle did for a living anyway?"

"He ran an extortion ring."

My eyebrows shot up. "Really. You come from a long line of hardened criminals."

"It's not funny, John."

"It is. Just a little bit. Are there any other big dark skeletons in your closet you're hiding?"

"No."

"Was your father part of it?"

"No, he wasn't," she snapped.

"Then why did he get out?" Knocker asked.

"Because people came looking for him to use as leverage against his brother. He only wanted to keep us safe."

"Do you remember anything about him?"

"Not a thing. Is that enough?"

I held up my hands in defense. "Hey, I'm just curious."

Holly's phone rang. She accepted the call, placing it on speaker so we could all hear. "Smith."

"Did you hear the news?" the woman's voice echoed around the room.

"We did."

"What do you intend to do about it?"

"Who is this?"

"Miriam Craig."

"Oh shit."

"It's fine, just relax. You've only talked to me once or twice, so it's quite understandable that you didn't recognize my voice over the phone. Now answer the question. What do you propose to do about it?"

"Ma'am, we have a lead in Brussels. We have a meeting with a man very soon who might have information on where we need to be."

"Nothing definite?" Miriam asked.

"No, ma'am, but we're hopeful."

"Hopeful isn't really good enough, Miss Smith."

"That's about all you'll get, ma'am," Holly replied.

"Then I guess it'll have to do. Keep me updated."

"Yes, ma'am."

The line went dead as the call disconnected. Holly looked at me. "Talk about pressure."

"A super nuke will do that," I replied. "But don't worry. What's the worst thing that could happen?"

"Great. Just as it goes off, I'll think, wow, what's the worst that could happen?"

"Fine. You'll die comforted."

"Asshole."

———

Noah Smets was in his sixties, his hair gray, and his skin a roadmap of lines and gullies. He stared at Holly and said, "You look like your mother."

"You look like shit," Holly replied casually.

"Twenty years in this place will do that to you," he said. His gaze fell on me. "Who is the Titan?"

"A friend."

Placed in a room on our own, not even a guard was present. I guess they figured everything was safe with someone my size facing off against an old man. I said, "My name is John."

"Good. Now we have the niceties out of the way. What do you want, girl?"

"We need your help."

The old man raised an inquisitive eyebrow while looking at me and smiled. "I have seen nothing of my family for thirty years, yet now they want my help."

"I can't help that."

His eyes traveled back to Holly. "What do you want my help with? Tell me and I will see if I want to play with you."

"This is not a fucking game, uncle," Holly whispered harshly. "Millions of lives could depend on it."

He folded his arms and leaned back in his seat, smiling to reveal crooked yellow teeth. "So overdramatic, girl. Yes, you are your mother's daughter."

"Screw you."

"And there is your father. I see you got the best of both worlds."

"Are you going to help us or not?" Holly snarled.

"You still haven't told me what you want to know."

"We're looking for Jan Witsel."

"Who?"

"You know who I mean," Holly said. "Even though you're locked in here, you are not without connections."

Smets leaned forward. "How would you know that? Have you been keeping tabs on me?"

"I don't have time to play games, Noah."

"What is in it for me?" he asked.

"How long do you have left?" Holly asked.

"Five years."

"Fine. Tell us what we want to know, and you'll be out tomorrow."

Smets looked skeptical. "How do I know you can do that?"

"Because I can. I work for MI6."

"Wow. You're a big girl now." The sarcasm in his voice was almost tangible.

"Where can we find Jan Witsel?"

He nodded. "You will need to give me an hour. I will call you when I know."

"You'd better not be messing us around, Noah," Holly cautioned him.

"I can find out for you. You just make sure I'm out of here tomorrow. I have things to do."

Holly left a number with the warden. Once we were outside, I asked her, "Do you think he can do it?"

"I think so."

"What is he in for anyway?" I asked.

"He murdered his best friend."

"Why would he do that?"

Holly stopped. "The guy turned police informant. Noah found out and cut his heart out. It was a warning against any of the others who might turn against him."

"He got twenty-five years for that?"

"He did."

"Do you think he's reformed?"

Her face turned hard like granite. "If he hasn't, I'll

know about it. Then I'll come over here and put a bullet in his head myself. Come on."

———

The call came through exactly an hour later. Holly answered to hear Noah's gravelly voice on the other end. "You will find him under the Belfry Theater."

"Under?" Holly asked.

"Yes, that's what I said."

"Why there?"

"Because he's a wanted man. That's why he changes location all the time. I have it on good authority that he'll be there for the next twenty-four hours. After that, he's in the wind again."

"I hope you're right."

"What about our deal?" the old man asked.

"Expect to be moved tomorrow."

The call disconnected and I turned to Slick. "What are we dealing with?"

"No idea. The Belfry has been shut down for a long time. If there is something underneath it, I don't know about it."

"Then we'll just have to take a swing at it and hope we hit," I said.

So, that was what we did. Gearing up, we left for the theater.

———

From the outside, it appeared dilapidated and was fenced off with temporary fencing. Each panel had warning signs for trespassers to keep out. Doing a final check on our weapons, we ensured we had what we needed. The sun was still up but making its way toward the horizon which meant we were making a daylight incursion. A rear alley was where we had chosen to breach, away from prying eyes.

While Holly and Slick remained in the van, we went in through the back door as quietly as possible. No sooner had we entered than we found our first hurdle. As luck would have it, he was fast asleep in a chair. Making the choice to leave him there instead of killing him, we crept past and went further into the theater. Our aim was to get beneath somehow, so when we found a set of rickety wooden stairs, we took them.

They led us down into a junk-filled basement. Old props and costumes littered the space. Looking around, there was nothing to indicate what we sought.

"Where the fuck do we go from here?"

"No idea," I replied. "There must be something somewhere. Why else have an armed guard at the back door?"

Suddenly, we heard footsteps coming down the basement stairs. We stepped back into the shadows and prepared for contact.

The armed man appeared and was gone. He walked through a large rack of costumes and coats and vanished.

"Did you check that?" I asked Knocker.

"Did you?" he shot back at me.

Beyond the racks was a closed doorway. I tried the knob, and it opened smoothly. Beyond it were cata-combs that looked to have once been air raid shelters.

Now they were something else. An underground mansion and the home of a very rich man.

One who was expecting us. Facing our direction with automatic weapons were six heavily armed men. Knocker spat on the floor. "Well, that's fucked."

Suddenly a voice boomed over a public address system. "Welcome, Mr. Kane, Mr. Jensen. Please, follow my men and they will bring you to me. You have nothing to fear. If I wanted you dead, you would already be so."

I looked at Knocker. "What would you say?"

"Bollocks."

"That will do it."

———

We were escorted to what amounted to a large open plan apartment underground by three guards. Witsel was reclined on a leather lounge, drinking gin, a Doberman at his feet. To top it off, he was clad in a luxurious robe.

"Welcome, gentlemen." His English was quite good, even though it held a hint of an accent. "I have been expecting you."

"Seems to be the trend lately," Knocker said.

The transporter gave a nod of acceptance. "Your reputation precedes you. From what I have heard, you are both quite capable men. It makes me wish that I had you on my side."

"Why are we here?" I asked.

"Not for me to kill you, as I said before. Which is why you were allowed to keep your weapons."

"That's mighty generous of you," I replied.

"I thought so."

"Are you going to speak, or what?" Knocker asked.

"You are here because of a package I delivered for a client. Let me preface what I'm about to say by telling you I had no idea what it was. People in our—"

"Get on with it," I said. "We had this conversation recently."

"I was approached by a Russian a while back asking me to transport a package. He was offering twenty million to see it done. I agreed."

"Igoshin or Morozov?" I asked.

"The first meeting was with Morozov. The second was when the package came. That was Grigori Igoshin. There had been a change of plan. They wanted me to store the package until they were ready for it to be delivered."

"Didn't that strike you as odd?" I asked.

"Very. But they put up another twenty million, so I didn't ask questions. They even supplied security for it."

"You weren't curious?" Knocker asked.

Witsel shook his head. "No. Like I said, no questions."

"What changed?"

He stared at me. "They told me you would be coming and that I should kill you on sight."

Knocker moved first and I wasn't far behind him. Our Glocks came up and around, taking the three guards behind us by surprise. Our handguns fired almost continuously as we took all three down with multiple shots. They were all dead as they hit the concrete floor.

We spun back and pointed the weapons at Witsel. "How did you know?"

"From experience," I replied.

"They have been holding me here for days, waiting. They were to kill me if I went against Igoshin's wishes. It was then that I realized something terrible was about to happen. What is it?"

"A super nuke."

"I feared as much."

"When did it leave?"

"Two days ago."

"Where to?"

"London."

"Where in London?"

"I do not know," Witsel replied. "It could be anywhere."

I said into my comms, "Holly, did you get all that?"

"Roger."

Turning back to Witsel, I said, "Be seeing you around."

He held up his drink in a salute. "Good luck."

"Yeah."

My next call once we reached the van was to Miriam Craig. She answered by saying, "I'm guessing you have bad news, otherwise you wouldn't call."

"The bomb is in London," I told her.

"Where?"

"That's something we don't know. But don't jump the gun. Let us do our thing."

"You expect me to do nothing? Is that what you're saying?"

"Just let us take care of it. You start having all your

intelligence companies stomping around London and something is bound to go wrong."

"Do not presume to tell me what to do, Mr. Kane."

"Wouldn't dream of it, ma'am."

"I'll think it over."

And she did. For about five minutes. Then she put all her intelligence people onto it. And made our job that much harder.

CHAPTER 16

"OF ALL THE STUPID FUCKING BULLSHIT THINGS TO DO," Knocker shouted.

I shook my head. Holly had just broken the news to us from the MOD that an alert had gone out from the Prime Minister's office about the nuke. We had arrived back in London just after midnight, and now that it was morning, we had to find the nuke before someone fucked up and initiated a catastrophe of epic proportions.

We were in a hangar at Brize Norton that had been set aside for us to use as an operations center, along with some help from military intelligence. Everything we needed had been provided, now all we had to do was find something we could use. Difficult, you might say. But we had Slick, and the man was a bloody genius.

"Paddy O'Malley," Slick said.

"Who?" I asked.

"Paddy O'Malley. Used to be in with several IRA splinter groups."

"How far in?" Knocker asked. "And how can he help?"

"He used to run arms for them. He may be old, but he still knows things."

"How do you know that?" I asked.

"Because I just talked to someone who knows," Slick replied evasively.

"Where might we find him?"

"The Irish Arms pub. I'll text you the address. It opens at eleven, but he's always there from nine."

"Is there anything we should know about it?" I asked.

"No, just watch your backs."

"Great."

———

Taking one of the black SUVs supplied for our use, we drove through the busy London traffic until we found the pub. As luck would have it, there was a vacant park across the road, which we pulled into. Securing our Glocks in the SUV's glove compartment, we climbed out and locked it. We'd chosen to go in unarmed to save trouble and bloodshed. Knocker pushed the heavy door open, and we walked inside.

"We're not open yet," the barman called over to us.

The barroom smelled of stale alcohol and carpet deodorizer. The place was well lit and there were three other people inside at the bar.

I said, "We're looking for Paddy O'Malley."

"Never heard of him," the barman replied.

I glanced at the others. "How about you?"

They ignored us.

My eyes focused on the oldest one there. "How about you, old man?"

His face seemed to harden despite the weathered skin and deep lines. "Who the fuck are you calling, old man?"

"No offense meant," I replied. "But if you're Paddy, then we need to talk to you."

"I'm not him," he said firmly.

Knocker took out a photo we'd been supplied with, holding it out to show the man his image. "Are you sure? You kind of look a lot like him."

"Torture squad bastard," the old man snarled at Knocker. "You have the stink all over you."

"Fuck off, bogtrotter. You have no idea what I am."

"Now we have the pleasantries out of the way, are you going to talk to us or not?" I asked the Irishman. "Millions of lives do depend on it."

"I think you'd better piss off," the barman said firmly.

The other two men rose from their barstools and started forward. A small but audible sigh escaped Knocker's lips before he acted. A right fist streaked forward, followed by a left, then a right elbow.

The Irish thug went down hard and never moved. Knocker said, "His jaw's broken. He'll need a doctor."

"And you'll need a coffin," the barman said, standing there with a sawn-off shotgun pointed at us.

I held both hands at shoulder level. "Just take it easy. All we wanted was to come here and talk. We have a situation that we need help with." I turned my gaze back to O'Malley. "Something you might be able to help us with to save a lot of lives."

The old man stared at me. "Speak."

"A few days ago, a package was brought into London. Did you hear anything about it?"

"You'll have to be more specific."

"It was sent here by Jan Witsel. Some Russians came with it."

"What's in it for me?" he asked.

"Not a thing," I replied honestly.

"Then I heard nothing."

"Listen, old man," Knocker snapped. "We don't have time for your shit. There is a nuclear device somewhere in London and we need to find it before it goes bloody boom."

That got his attention. He glanced at me. I nodded. "It's true."

"The receiver was Danny Frost. Find him and you'll get answers."

"Is that it?"

O'Malley nodded. "That's all I know."

"Where do we find him?" I asked.

"He usually hangs out at Barney's, over in the East End."

"What's Barney's?" Knocker asked.

"It's a front for a prostitution ring. It's a restaurant with a hidden menu. People go there for lunch and dinner and can choose something from both menus."

"Does he own it?"

"Danny?" O'Malley seemed to find humor in the question. "Fuck no. The bastard just goes there and blows all his money on the girls. It's owned by Lenny Morris. He's someone you will need to watch out for."

I nodded. "Thanks for your help."

"When you see Danny," O'Malley said, "punch him in the mouth for me."

This was beginning to resemble a game of catch. We were hopping from one point to another, and yet the prize seemed to be always just out of reach. We got back into the SUV and headed to Barney's, an establishment that was a different proposition altogether.

Our last foray had gone relatively smoothly. This one didn't. Not at all.

———

Barney's was a good setup overall. The restaurant was clean and looked normal. It was open all day for lunch and dinner. The clientele was well dressed, as were the women who worked there. Nothing overt or scantily clad but dressed to catch the eye in a respectable way. I guess that's how they got away with it.

The men who patronized the place had to select a woman from the menu before they were shown to a table, the ordered young lady joining them soon after. They would have lunch or dinner together before things progressed from there.

When Knocker and I entered, we were met in the reception area by a well-dressed man. He looked us up and down before asking, "Do you have a reservation, sirs?" We obviously didn't resemble their usual clientele.

I shook my head. "Sorry."

"Then I can't help you, I'm afraid."

Knocker produced a couple hundred in bills. "Are you sure you couldn't find us a table?"

The concierge looked at the money and swallowed. "We—we might be able to find something for you."

"Good man."

He reached for a leather-bound folder that said Menu. I opened it and saw the face of a young woman staring back at me, her hair and lipstick dark. "What's this?"

"You need a dining companion, sir."

"Really?"

"Yes, sir. It is part of the rules."

I flicked through the plastic sleeves and stopped at a blonde woman, tapping my index finger on his picture. "What about her?"

"Excellent choice, sir. Adrianne would be my choice. I think she is available."

I passed the folder to Knocker. "Here you go, Charlie, make your choice."

He turned two pages and said, "Her."

The woman was black. "Ah, yes, Heather. A wise choice. Follow me and I will show you to a table. Or perhaps you would like a booth?"

Can't see anything from a booth. "A table will be fine."

He said, "Please, follow me."

Stepping from behind the reception counter, he led us to a table and said, "The ladies will be with you directly."

He disappeared and Knocker picked up the menu. "Three, one, and eleven."

I nodded. "Six and nine."

"Seems to be a lot of security."

"We were warned."

"Should have come bearing gifts, Reaper."

I looked down at the flatware on the table in front of us. "We'll manage."

A few minutes later, our ladies joined us. Heather

was British with a heavy cockney accent, while Adrianne's voice suggested she'd originated from Eastern
Europe. We bought them a drink and ordered meals.
Small talk lasted a little longer than the time it took to
order. I said, "We heard of this place from a friend of
ours. Says he comes here all the time."

"Who might that be, love?" Heather asked.

"Danny Frost? Know him?"

A flicker in her eyes told me she did. But still, she
lied. "No."

"Are you sure? He says he comes here all the
time."

"No."

I looked at Adrianne. "You?"

"No, not me. I know nothing."

"Are you sure?"

"I need to go to the bathroom," Heather said.

"Me too," Adrianne decided.

We watched them go and knew what was coming.
Minutes later, a man flanked by two bigger men
stepped up to the table. He said, "My name is Lenny
Morris. I hear you've been causing trouble."

Morris was in his forties and wore a black suit. His
hair was slicked back, and he had a pencil-thin
mustache like that of a thirties gangster. I said, "Nope,
not us. We were asking about a friend."

"How about you come with me, and we can
discuss it further in my office."

"I think we're fine."

"It wasn't a request," he said.

One of the men opened their suit jacket to flash the
butt of a handgun. I nodded. "Okay, let's do that."

We were escorted into Morris's office and got a

surprise when we arrived. Danny Frost was waiting for us. Not that we knew him at the time. "Now," Morris said, "tell me who you are looking for."

"Frosty the snowman," Knocker said.

One of the bodyguards hit him in the lower back and he buckled at the knees. Through gritted teeth, Knocker said, "Do it again, and I'll peel your fucking ears off."

He did it again. Knocker straightened and said, "Right, you were warned."

"Enough," Morris barked. "What do you want with Danny?"

"Yeah, what do you want with me?"

I stared at him. He didn't seem to have enough brains to make a mess if he'd been shot in the head with a shotgun. "You received a package from across the channel along with some passengers. I need to know where they are."

"No, I didn't," Frost denied.

"Yes. Listen, we need to know where they are."

"Who do you work for?" Morris asked.

"That doesn't matter."

"Yes, it does. It decides whether or not you get out of here alive."

"We work for the British government," Knocker said.

Morris nodded at his first man. He made to pull his handgun, but I reacted quicker than he figured I could. My left hand clamped down on the wrist reaching for his weapon. My bunched right fist smashed him hard in the face and he dropped like the proverbial stone.

His friend went for his own weapon and Knocker was already moving. He hit him in the throat and brought him to his knees. Then, using his own knee, Knocker brought it up and smashed the security guy in the face. I heard the jaw break, and he fell onto his side, out cold. Knocker picked up the gun and pointed it at Morris. "Now, if you give us a chance to explain, you'll see exactly why that was uncalled for."

"I don't give a shit, mate," he hissed. "I ever see you again, I'll kill the pair of you."

Shaking his head, Knocker said, "I do wish you had not said that."

"Don't kill him. Not yet." I turned my attention to Frost. I walked over to him and had the sudden thought that, for a hardened criminal, he wasn't overly brave. I grabbed him by the nose and twisted. "Where did you take them?"

"The bunker," he blurted out.

"What bunker?"

"The one under Downing Street."

"The PM's bunker?" Knocker asked.

"No, there's another one there that dates back to World War Two. It's the old living quarters and operations rooms that Churchill stayed in when he was there during the Blitz."

"That was under Whitehall," Knocker said.

"Yes, there was one there, but there was also this one."

"How big is the complex?"

"Big enough."

"How do we get in there?" I asked.

"Via a doorway behind Mountbatten Green. You get in there."

"How many Russians?"

"Four."

"Do you have any idea what they have?" Knocker asked.

"No, I didn't ask anything," Frost said.

"Maybe you should have," I said. "Come on, we're leaving."

"Don't you want to know about the other men?"

Suddenly, the sound of automatic gunfire erupted from within the restaurant. I glanced at Knocker, who shook his head. "Fucking bollocks."

I grabbed the handgun from the unconscious security guy at my feet and straightened up. "I'll be glad when this is fucking over."

Knocker and I hurried toward the office door. I opened it and saw a clear hallway in front of us. For a moment at least. That was until a shooter appeared with an AK. "Get back!" I shouted, slamming the door.

7.62mm rounds shredded the thin wood as they punched through it. Frost jerked as a bullet found flesh, then a second. "I'm hit. I—"

Two more and he died where he sat.

Morris had ducked down behind his desk. I looked at Knocker, who'd pressed himself against the wall. He shrugged. Never spoke, just let his shoulders rise and fall.

There was a pause and I immediately threw the door open. The shooter was reloading. The handgun I took from the security guy fired twice and the bullets hit the man in the chest. He staggered and I fired two more times.

By the time I reached him, he was down and dead. I grabbed his AK-12 and finished reloading it. Then I went out into the restaurant.

At first, I made three shooters, but there were more than that. They were randomly shooting anyone who moved, creating confusion and chaos. There was no reason to do so, but they were. I brought the AK around and sighted the first shooter I came across.

My finger stroked the trigger, and I reeled in shock as a civilian took a round to the head.

"You opened fire in a crowded room and shot a civilian?" Holland shouted at me. *"What kind of fool are you?"*

"One trying to stop the massacre of innocent people."

"How did that work out?"

"Fine."

As the man fell, I saw the handgun in his hand. Then I realized what was happening. They had people in the restaurant waiting for us. Once we'd been seen, they called in the rest. I shouted at Knocker. "They've got people inside the wire."

"Fuck."

I ducked back behind a concrete pillar responsible for supporting the weight of the ceiling. People were still dying. As I searched for a new target, I saw a woman in a sleek dress spin and fall, a blotch of red between her breasts.

I found another target and fired. This time, I hit what I aimed at, and he fell into the throng of moving people.

"Reaper, look out!"

The shout made me turn to see a man in a suit no more than four feet from where I stood, with a handgun pointed at my head. I was dead to rights. He had me cold. Then his skull exploded in a blast of blood and brain matter as a bullet from Knocker ended his life.

Bullets came my way from another shooter, and I was forced back behind the pillar. Knocker was crouched behind a table, making the best of what little cover it supplied.

Bullets peppered my position and dug deep scars into the concrete. I shouted across at Knocker, "Cover me?"

"What for?"

"I'm going for the cubicle."

He looked past me and then shouted back, "Ten bucks says you don't get halfway."

"Screw you."

He rose and opened fire. "Go!"

I left the cover of the pillar and raced for the cubicle. When I was almost there, I threw myself the rest of the way. It was stupid and hurt like hell when I hit the table, but I was safe for the moment.

I was about to open fire again when I heard a woman's cry. Looking around, I saw that it was Heather. "Are you okay?" I asked her.

She pointed at the floor. When I looked, I saw Adrianne, eyes wide, a bullet hole in her forehead, blood pooling around her hair. I muttered a curse. With a deep growl, I fired at a target and missed. Ducking back, I regrouped and then tried again. This time, I was rewarded with the sight of the man falling.

We had no idea how many were left at that point. It was a well-coordinated attack and a well-planned trap. Many times over, throughout the war to stop the Russians, we should have died, yet by the skin of our teeth, we always managed to get through. If you put this stuff in a book, the reader would shake their head and say, "Yeah, right."

The AK rattled once more then stopped almost instantly. The charging handle was locked back. I threw it away and drew the handgun, checking the magazine so I would know roughly how many rounds were left. At that time, maybe half.

Not that I got to use it because a well-dressed killer chose that particular moment to throw himself at me. His hands grappled for my throat. My bunched fist hammered toward his face, but the blow glanced off his shoulder. My fist caught him in the side of the head and pain shot through my hand.

I felt my attacker's own fist strike me on the left cheek. He was on top of me, his face a mask of snarled hatred. I lashed out again, this time finding the killer's nose. It gave under the vicious blow, and he reeled back as blood started to flow.

When he rolled off me, it gave me the chance to bring the handgun into play. I drove it hard into his middle and pulled the trigger three times. He doubled over and grunted. Then I placed the gun against his head and fired a fourth.

I came up to my knees. Across the way, Knocker had stopped firing. I looked at him and he signaled he was out of ammo.

I saw him reach into his pocket. "Oh, fuck no."

"Don't even think about it," I called over to him.

He gave me a questioning look. "What?"

Knocker was holding a knife. I felt a sudden wave of relief wash over me. Many a time in the past, a grenade had made a miraculous appearance. It was about now that I realized that the gunfire had ceased. Just stopped cold.

That was when the police arrived. And we were arrested.

————

We were placed in the rear seat of separate police vehicles. When the detective inspector came back, I said to him, "I need to make a call."

"Not fucking likely, mate," he growled.

A young woman stood beside him, a detective sergeant named Grace. "Do you realize how many bodies you dropped in there?"

"The only bodies we dropped were the bad guys," I replied.

"What bad guys?" she asked.

"The Russians."

The DI shook his head. "I don't know which is worse. Your answer or your fucking mate's."

"What did he say?" I asked.

"That the bloody Wombles did it."

I shook my head. "What a dick. You wouldn't find Wombles around here. It was Dougal from the Magic Roundabout."

"Is this bloody funny to you?"

I shook my head. "No, it's dead serious. Now let me make that fucking call."

"No, sit there—"

Another detective appeared. "Boss, you need to come and look at this."

The detectives gave me a serious glower with an unspoken warning to not give his people any grief, then disappeared inside the restaurant while I was left to watch the throng of onlookers, police, and reporters.

They returned five minutes later. The DI held out his cell and showed me a picture. It was a tattoo. A star and sickle. "Three of the bodies you dropped in there had these tattoos. I'm guessing there are more on the others."

I stared at the photo.

"Nothing to say?" the DS asked.

"What do you want me to say?"

"Do you know what they mean?"

"Something to do with the fact they're Russian mercenaries," I told her.

"Why are Russian mercenaries in London?"

"Now you're asking the right question," I shot back at her.

"How about you answer the bloody question," the DI said.

"Because there is a nuke in London, that's why."

"The one we were alerted to?"

"Yes."

"Why are they after you?"

"Because we've been after them for a long time, and now we're getting close."

"Bullshit."

"Hey, Orinoco, can you hear me?"

"Sure can," Knocker called back.

I said, "Tell Cracker and Vera why we're in London."

"Because we like the warm beer."

"Now tell them the truth."

"Nuclear bomb."

I looked at them. "Now, give me that bloody phone call."

CHAPTER 17

I WAS GRATEFUL THAT THE CALL WORKED OUT, AND ONCE more, we were free to go our merry, chaotic way. We were briefing Holly on what had happened, when she informed us that she needed to call the PM.

"No," Knocker and I snapped together. "We do this on our own."

"We can't just do—"

"Yes, we can," Knocker said. "I kept secrets from her all the time when we were married."

"Damn it—"

"Call her when we go in. Not before," I said. "The last thing we want is her dropping a bloody great anvil of security people on top of us before we can do anything."

"Fine. It's against my better judgments, but we'll do it that way."

———

Arriving at Mountbatten Green in the middle of the night, we climbed from the van in our combat gear and armed with Heckler and Koch G36C compact carbines. Slick had already killed all electronic signals within a two-kilometer radius. He said, "You're not going to have much time before they realize that something is happening. It will stop any remote detonation, but if they're down there with it, then I'm afraid we're pretty much fucked."

"I love your optimism, Slick," I said to him. "It's been great knowing you."

Using the cover of darkness, we reached the door and tried the handle. It snicked open to reveal a stairwell extending down away from us. Taking what might be our final glimpse of the outside world, we headed down the steps fifty feet below the city.

In this dimly lit space, the silence was a heavy mantle on our shoulders, thick like the dust that coated every surface. Once a safe haven from the violence that had raged above during World War Two, the bunker now bore the weight of forgotten time. The air was cool, carrying the faint scent of damp stone and rusted metal. Walls of reinforced concrete stretched endlessly into the shadows, their once-pristine surfaces now mottled with patches of mildew and scars.

Faint rays of light filtered through narrow air vents high above, casting thin, pale beams across the concrete floor. They illuminated the skeletal remains of long-abandoned furniture, steel cots with sagging wireframes, a lone chair tilted awkwardly against the wall. The metal door, once a formidable barrier against air raids, stood slightly ajar. All of this was designed to give the impression of neglect, but we knew differently.

Knocker, in the lead, opened the door further and it groaned on its hinges. He slipped through, and for a moment, I lost him until I made the passage myself.

Beyond the doorway, the remnants of a control room appeared eerily intact. Dust-covered dials and switches lined the walls, their faded labels hinting at a time when they were crucial to survival. An old rotary phone sat on a desk, the cord coiled and brittle. Maps of the city, yellowed and peeling, clung stubbornly to the walls, their edges curling in the underground humidity. The meticulous lines and red circles denoting bomb sites had long since faded into ghostly traces of ink, blending into the paper like forgotten memories.

As Knocker and I moved on, overhead, pipes and wires ran along the ceiling, some sagging from their mounts, others still securely fastened. A faint drip echoed from somewhere in the labyrinth of the bunker's corridors. It was a rhythmic sound that could have come from a slow leak in the pipes or from the remnants of London's perpetual rain filtering down into the earth.

As we crept closer, the previous stillness of the bunker was interrupted by the faint hum of electronics. Hidden deep within the maze of corridors, in a space once sealed by thick steel blast doors, was a room now illuminated by the harsh, sterile light of portable lamps.

We sidled forward and saw a group of Russian mercenaries, Igoshin at their center, working methodically around an open crate. They moved carefully, their eyes sharp and focused, clad in tactical gear that glinted dully under the cold light. The room, once a storage area for ration crates, now served a far more sinister purpose.

The crate, which I guessed held the nuclear weapon we so desperately sought, sat in the center of the room. A low, ominous hum came from the device, and the faint red glow of a small control panel pulsed like a heartbeat, reflecting from the clothing of those who stood around it.

I looked at Knocker and used hand signals to relay the plan. We needed to execute it swiftly and with great precision.

One of the mercenaries, his face scarred and hard, stood beside the weapon, glancing frequently at a clipboard filled with notes in Russian. I heard him say, "Grigori, it is almost done."

"Good. Once the call comes through, we will start the timer."

"One minute?" It was a question, not a statement.

Igoshin nodded. "Yes. Mother Russia will remember us for this night. When President Lash, makes the announcement that all negotiations have broken down, then he will call. Get the rest of the wires."

Igoshin's comrades moved silently around him, looking for the wires required. The man who passed them to him said, "This thing is a fucking dinosaur, Grigori. Are we sure it will work?"

"It will work, Comrade."

For the duration of this conversation, we could hear the soft, steady beeps emitted from the weapon's control panel.

There were more men present than expected. Apart from those working on the bomb, there were four guards, all heavily armed. I tapped Knocker and held up two fingers and pointed left. Then I held up the same two and pointed at me then to the right. He nodded.

I heard Igoshin say, "Is there anything on the cameras we placed that should cause a problem?"

"No. Everything looks fine."

The wonders of Slick, I said inwardly.

As they finished up, the mercenaries spoke in low, clipped tones, their words sharp and efficient. They worked quickly, knowing that time was not on their side. Igoshin, his cold blue eyes flickering with both determination and the weight of expectation, glanced at the timer on the nuclear device. For a man who was facing imminent death, he was remarkably calm, as were his men.

During all of this, I suddenly became acutely aware that the dripping sound had ceased in anticipation of the devastation about to be perpetrated.

I held up my hand and counted down. When my fist clenched, we moved.

As we'd already agreed, I went right and Knocker went left. The suppressed G36C in my hands became a tool of death as I killed the first armed mercenary and then the second. On my left, Knocker did the same, and within seconds, four Russians lay in various crumpled positions on the cold concrete floor.

I heard a cry of alarm and swung my weapon around. One of the remaining Russians had a handgun out and loosed a shot in my direction. It failed to make contact but then ricocheted off the concrete wall with a deadly screech.

Once again, I squeezed the trigger, and a 5.56mm round punched into the man's chest. His body armor stopped the bullet cold, but it gave me time to shoot him in the head.

Having less trouble than me, Knocker put down another merc, which left only two.

Knocker shot the second to last one, leaving only Igoshin. There was a snarl of rage on his face as he lurched for something behind the crate containing the weapon. As he went down, I shot him twice.

Falling to the floor, he began squirming in pain. Keeping the G36C trained on the mercenary leader, I hurried forward. He looked up at me, blood covered his chest and his lips. "You cannot stop it," he managed to say.

"Don't be so sure," I said and shot him in the head.

I looked at the bomb and saw the counter running down. "Fuck."

The thought of imagining myself in such a situation had never crossed my mind: deep beneath London, in a bunker built to withstand bombs, now standing in front of one. My hands were starting to sweat despite the cold. The air in the underground room was thick with dust. I leaned over the nuclear device, its casing matte black. The timer on the bomb read 00:13:46. I could almost feel the seconds slipping away.

"At least it wasn't the short amount of time they'd been discussing, Reaper," Knocker said.

I nodded. "Yeah, we have ample time to get this done. What do you think?"

"It's old."

"Is that it?"

"What about you? What do you think?"

Focus.

The bunker's silence made every sound feel louder than it should have been. The soft click of my knife, the shallow rhythm of my breathing. I wiped my brow with the back of my hand, my fingers trembling as I fumbled with the cover panel, trying to pry it open. There was a satisfying pop as it came loose, revealing the tangle of wires that had just recently been placed.

"Haven't you trained for shit like this?" I asked Knocker.

"Nothing like this," he replied.

When I was with Global, I'd trained for this. Simulations, diagrams, drills that were all supposed to prepare me for exactly this moment. But those drills never felt like this, with the weight of an entire city above me. And that number ticking down, this one, unlike the ones I practiced on, would go boom as soon as the timer hit zero.

00:11:37.

"Come on, Reaper, you got this. I've seen you in those simulations. Red hot you were. You—"

"Shut up," I snapped. "What are you doing?"

"Moral support."

"You're making my ears bleed."

"That's probably the radiation."

I smiled as sweat dripped from my nose. "Dickhead."

I heard a distant creak, the old pipes, or maybe a loose ceiling panel. Unnatural sounds like that didn't help the situation much. It was like being on a plane when you were afraid to fly and picking up every change in the motor.

Focus. My entire world was the bomb in front of me. The wires were a mess of colors—red, blue, green, yellow, white, and they were intertwined like mating snakes. Some were clearly decoys. Which ones were real? Which ones would kill me? I stared at them, my mind flashing through training manuals and past missions.

"Fuck it, I'll just shoot it," I said, grabbing for my Glock.

Knocker grabbed my arm. "Just hold on a moment. That might not be such a good idea this time around."

I traced my finger along the yellow wire. "Could be the primary trigger. What do you think?"

Knocker shook his head. "Could be a trick designed to buy time. Or not. I've only defused a nuclear device once before. It was a lot different than this."

"Christ."

I looked at the timer.

00:09:55.

"Here goes," I said.

I cut the yellow wire. The sharp snip of the wire cutters was deafening in the empty room. There was a pause as if the bomb itself was waiting, deciding. The timer kept ticking. Good sign. Bad sign.

Knocker released a long, slow breath, and so did I. I didn't realize I was holding it at the time. Next, I looked at the blue wire. "Is that connected to a secondary system? Maybe it's a failsafe."

My eyes scanned the wiring. I suddenly realized that I'd seen this setup before in pictures when I'd done my training. They had said it was their *just-in-case* program. It was an old Russian design. Only difference was the scale—when they'd made it, it was made bigger. But here it was, hidden beneath layers of concrete in a city oblivious to the threat, full of people who thought they'd seen the worst the world could offer.

The timer was now down to 00:06:12. My hands moved faster, cutting, isolating circuits, checking for any hidden traps. It was all muscle memory. Knocker watched on, ready to stop me if he thought something wasn't right. Every decision had to be precise. Every snip of the cutter, every wire I moved out of the way. It all had to be exact.

Time seemed to dissolve.

00:03:48.

Apparently, I wasn't going as fast as I thought.

"Can you go any slower?" Knocker asked.

"Shut up."

"I would, but right now, you're killing me along with millions of others."

I was almost there. Sweat dripped down my face, and my heart thudded in my ears. I pulled back the last section of the panel to reveal the final trigger mechanism.

"Shit."

"Pressure mechanism," Knocker said.

"Yeah. They've rigged this thing to blow the second someone tries to tamper with it."

"The pin," Knocker said.

I looked up at him. "I thought you said you didn't know anything about these?"

"I lied. I didn't want you blaming me for killing us both."

00:01:17

"Asshole."

I closed my eyes for a moment, making sure I was composed for the next move. I had one chance. My fingers moved carefully, feeling for the tiny, almost invisible pin hidden inside the mechanism.

"I can't feel it."

00:00:58

"It has to be there."

"No shit."

00:00:47

I kept feeling around. "Got it."

Trying to grasp the small protrusion to pull it out, my fingers slipped off it. I closed my eyes, waiting for us to disappear into nuclear dust, but nothing happened. Across from me, Knocker was holding his breath, his eyes closed, his fingers in his ears.

00:00:17

Trying again, my fingers began to pull the pin free with excruciating slowness. There was a barely audible click, but in the silence, we both heard it. I hoped it wasn't the trigger mechanism.

I looked at the timer.

00:00:03

00:00:02

It stopped.

For a moment, I stood staring at the bomb. Then I realized it was over. The tension in my chest began to ease. Across from me, Knocker opened an eye. "Are we dead?"

"No."

"What?"

"Take your fingers out of your ears."

"I can't hear you."

I grabbed his left hand and pulled it away from his head. "We're alive."

"Thank bloody hell for that."

"Let's get up and I'll call Holly. Tell her that we've secured the threat."

Knocker looked at the nuke. "Yeah, with my luck, I'll get bloody radiation poisoning if I hang around here."

———

"All indicators are it would have gone boom this time around," Holly said. "You did well."

"I don't think I've ever sweated so much in my life," I replied.

"Where has it been taken?" Knocker asked.

Holly shrugged. "I didn't ask. They took it to wherever they take these things to be disposed of."

The beer on the table in front of me looked good, and I reached out to pick it up. We were in the back room of a pub, away from prying eyes, where we could relax. However, Slick looked edgy. Knocker slapped him on the shoulder, "Relax. Drink your beer and forget about everything for the time being."

He was about to say something when the door to the backroom opened, and Miriam Craig entered, flanked by her own personal security. "There they are. Britain's saviors."

I drank some of my beer.

"I just wanted to say well done. I should never

have doubted your capabilities of accomplishing the mission."

"Thanks, ma'am," Holly said.

"So, what next for you?"

"The job isn't done yet," I replied. "There are still two more men out there responsible for what happened. In addition to the mole in MI6."

"Hecate? Are you still on about that?"

"The mole is still out there," Knocker said.

"Leave it. You've had a victory. God knows you've been chasing this down for a long time. Let Five take over."

I stared at her. She nodded and said, "Okay, must go. Well done."

With that, she turned on her heel, exiting the room but leaving a distinct trace of perfume in her wake.

Knocker stared in my direction and said, "We're not stopping, are we?"

"No."

"Didn't think so."

"Okay, how do we play our hand now?" Holly asked.

"We find Morozov."

———

It took the better part of two weeks, but we finally found him. Knocker, Slick, and I were bobbing around Europe in the hope of locating something. In that time, Lash had gone quiet and surrounded himself with a battalion of handpicked men as bodyguards.

Each city we went to, we spent time finding and contacting shadowy underworld figures. Initially, we thought that Morozov had returned to Moscow. And we were right. He'd been there two days before flying back to Western Europe. He'd spent time in Berlin, Antwerp, Munich, Milan, and Amsterdam. But we caught up with him in Paris.

"He's at the embassy," Slick said.

"Have you worked out what he's been doing this past week?" I asked.

"He's been visiting expelled oligarchs."

"Now why would he be doing that?" Knocker asked.

I thought for a moment. "He's rallying support."

"What—oh. He's going to make a run at the top job. Get rid of Lash."

"That would explain all of the security Lash has engaged," Holly said. "And why Morozov is not hiding in Russia."

"Good," said Knocker. "Let them kill each other."

"Bad," I replied. "We need them both gone."

"Yes, but to get to Lash, we need to get into the Kremlin. To do that, we need to get into Moscow, and to do that, we need to get into Russia."

I nodded. "I might have a way."

Knocker stared at me long and hard, reading my mind. "Ah, shit."

CHAPTER 18

THE RUSSIAN EMBASSY SAT IN THE HEART OF PARIS. THE building, designed in a neoclassical style, had towering columns, which contributed to its beauty. The façade bore the double-headed eagle, the emblem of Russian sovereignty, casting a watchful gaze over all who entered.

Surrounding the embassy were meticulously maintained gardens and neatly trimmed hedges. When we entered, the heavy and ornate doors opened to reveal a marble-floored lobby.

The interior of the embassy exuded an atmosphere that seemed tense. Rich, dark wood paneling and plush velvet furnishings provided an inviting ambiance. Portraits of Russian leaders lined the walls, their eyes seeming to follow every movement within the walls.

The grand staircase stretched out before us, its intricate wrought-iron railing leading to a realm of covert operations and high-stakes diplomacy. Here, advanced technology worked silently behind the scenes.

The large windows offered views of the Parisian skyline, a tranquil backdrop to the embassy's operations against the West.

Knocker and I stopped in the lobby, waiting for something to happen. At first, we were eyed suspiciously by the staff and security. A few muted conversations followed, and then we found ourselves at the center of chaos, men with guns pointed in our direction ordering us to get on the ground.

Moments later, a familiar face appeared. "This is almost like every Christmas I ever wanted as a boy."

I stared at Morozov. "At least this one didn't go off with a bang. And you can cross Igoshin off your guest list."

"Grigori was a good soldier. Reliable and trustworthy. But we shall discuss it all later. Bring them." He gave a flip of his hand as he walked off, the expectation that his order would be followed closely.

We were taken downstairs into the basement, where we were locked away in a cell. Morozov said, "I will return soon. Then we shall talk more."

"Well, we're in," Knocker said.

I nodded. "I just hope that everyone else is awake."

———

When Morozov returned an hour later, he seemed inordinately pleased with himself. I said, "Is this where you tell us that you're going to kill us?"

He grinned. "No, alas, no. After all the disturbance you have made to our plans, the president and myself have determined that a public trial before the world media is warranted. Then we will kill you. Slowly."

"So, Moscow?"

"Yes, Moscow."

"You know, you might as well just give it all away," I said. "You're the only one left. Why not crawl off into the darkness somewhere and wait for death to come?"

"We will rebuild."

"And then what?" I asked. "You can't get past NATO. You already tried that. Stop living in the fucking past and embrace the future."

"You're talking about Pushkin? When we find him, he'll die like the rest. He is nothing but a western puppet."

"He sees the future for what it is."

Morozov ignored my words. He then said, "What I can't work out, is why you would just walk into the embassy knowing what would happen."

"Maybe we missed you," Knocker replied.

"Ah, the lap dog speaks."

Knocker continued. "Maybe we saw it as an opportunity to get close to you so we could cut your fucking heart out."

"You will not be making jokes for much longer because we leave for Moscow tomorrow. Enjoy your stay in our luxurious surroundings."

He left us to our lodgings for the evening.

———

As the helicopter descended, the military base outside Moscow emerged from the thick veil of late-season snow. From the air, it resembled a cold, sterile scar in the landscape, a cluster of squat, concrete buildings surrounded by high fences topped with barbed wire. Watchtowers stood at each corner, their silhouettes blurred in the swirling snow. A distant line of armored vehicles was barely visible through the white haze, parked in neat rows.

I glanced at Knocker and nodded. His was almost as imperceptible as mine. Morozov sat across from us.

The rotors kicked up a storm of ice and dirt as we touched down. The mercenaries didn't hesitate. As soon as the helicopter hit the ground, they motioned for us to move, their weapons aimed directly at us. I stepped out onto the hard-packed earth, the bitter cold immediately biting at the flesh of my face, my breath visible in short bursts of mist. The smell of diesel and oil hung heavy in the frigid air.

They took us toward the small convoy of armored vehicles at the edge of the landing pad, their engines idling, exhaust fumes adding to the thickening fog. In the background, soldiers moved with machine-like stiffness, loading crates, running checks, their faces obscured beneath layers of winter gear. Even though we were outsiders in their world, no one seemed to notice us beyond our escort.

The soldiers pushed us toward one of the armored vehicles, a hulking thing coated in a thin layer of snow, even as it sat idle. The door swung open with a heavy thud, and we were shoved inside. The interior smelled of sweat and metal, was dimly lit and cramped, the walls lined with instruments and weapons. It was cold. The vehicle's engine growled to life as the doors slammed shut behind us.

Moving off, the convoy began grinding its way

over the icy roads as we left the base behind. The drive was a blur of frost-covered landscapes, the world outside a frozen mass of trees and barren fields. Every few miles, we passed checkpoints, heavily armed soldiers peering into the convoy, checking, nodding. The outskirts of Moscow loomed in the distance, the dark shapes of the buildings on the horizon through the storm.

Moscow's edges were lined with more checkpoints, more security forces, but soon, the structures of the inner city came into view once again.

The rumble of the engine stopped as we pulled into a narrow alley. Outside, I caught my first uninterrupted glimpse of the new Moscow from the inside. The streets were gray, lined with towering buildings that seemed to lean inward, as if submitting to the weight of the sky. The thick winter air felt sharp in my lungs when we stepped out, flanked by two mercenaries whose faces were blank behind their dark visors. One gave me a slight nudge, urging me forward. I didn't look at them.

The streets were empty, eerily quiet, but I could sense unseen eyes on us. The mercenaries walked with quick, deliberate steps, their weapons hanging low but never relaxed. Each one moved as if anticipating a threat from every corner, though nothing stirred in the frozen city. Our boots echoed as we passed beneath the shadow of looming buildings, their facades worn. A dull light filtered through the overcast sky, washing everything in muted shades of gray.

Ahead, beneath the towering walls of the Kremlin, was a throng of people. It took me a moment to work out who they were, but then I realized. Reporters. Our international media display started here and now.

The crimson stone of the walls were almost hidden beneath the frost. The golden domes of the cathedrals peeked above the walls, layered in snow.

"I feel like I'm walking to the gallows," Knocker said to me in a low voice.

"I hope they're putting on afternoon tea," I replied.

"Fuck off. Vodka and chocolate."

"You're a sick man."

The gates opened and we were ushered inside amid the shouts and calls from the press. I caught Knocker giving them a big cheesy grin and heard him say, "Someone send me flowers for my grave."

The mercenaries closed ranks around us. There was no need for words, no need for explanation. We had known this moment was inevitable from the time we stepped into the Russian embassy in Paris. The guards posted along the walls remained motionless, their faces hidden behind layers of cloth keeping out the biting cold. Inside, the vast courtyard stretched out like a barren wasteland.

We were hurried along, the mercenaries tightening their grip on their weapons as we passed below arches and through corridors of thick stone.

———

Knocker and I were taken before Sergey Lash in an office that was a blend of imperial grandeur and modern architecture. I looked around the room, it was spacious, with high walls adorned with portraits of past Russian leaders and crests and national emblems.

A highly polished large mahogany desk dominated the center of the room. On its surface lay official papers, stacked in neat piles. And there was Lash, sitting in his ornate, high-backed chair with a look of triumph on his face.

"Do you know how long I have waited for this moment?" His voice was high-pitched with excitement.

Knocker said, "If you provide a pen, we'll sign autographs for you. What do you think, Reaper?"

I nodded. "Sure. Something like *having a great time, wish you were dead*."

Knocker shook his head. "Too many words. I was thinking along the lines of, *suck my dick*."

"That will work."

"Enough," Morozov snapped.

"Let them make their jokes, Genady. Soon they will be in the most horrific environment on the planet. We'll see how they like it there."

"I thought we had decided on having them shot after their trial."

"I have changed my mind. We will send them to Smert."

And there it was. I saw for the first time that Morozov wasn't impressed at being overridden by his boss. Their relationship was already quite strained, and all we needed was a catalyst to take it to breaking point. Time to add a little tension.

"Did you enjoy your trip from Paris?" Lash asked.

"Not as much as Genady enjoyed his whirlwind tour of Western Europe," I replied.

"What are you talking about?"

"Ask Genady. He's been out rallying the oligarchs."

Lash stared at the general. "He talks nonsense," Morozov said to his boss.

"Really? You were gone for a while."

"Just on business, Sergey. Nothing more."

"Lock them up. They will go on trial tomorrow."

"What for?" I asked.

"For the murder of General Mikhail Shatov."

Morozov nodded. He waved his hand, and the guards moved in to escort us out. But as we left, I saw the hint of distrust in Lash's eyes as he concentrated on every move Morozov made.

———

The courtroom was packed with press. Most were Russian State press, but there was a smattering of foreign press reporters present as well.

The room was a high-ceilinged rectangular prism, the walls painted in neutral tones, mostly beige, and lined with wood paneling for a traditional feel. Large windows let in a dim natural light, reflecting the day outside. Overcast, solemn.

At the front of the room was a dais with the presiding judge's bench. Behind it was the Russian coat of arms, a two-headed eagle, displayed prominently. To the left and right of the judge were the places for court clerks, with a Russian flag standing tall to one side. The bench was made of dark wood, and a microphone was fixed in front of the judge for clear communication.

As we were ushered in, a thin man with a bald

head called out to us, "Mr. Kane, Mr. Jensen, we are doing all we can to get you out."

The man's name was Richards. A sports attaché, he was tasked with trying to get us free. Or was going through the motions anyway. At the moment, we were right where we wanted to be.

We sat down at the defense table with our show trial lawyer. He was a Russian officer in plain clothes. Put there to make things appear as though justice was being served. We looked around and waited for the judge to appear.

Our *lawyer* leaned over and said in a hushed voice. "You will not speak or make a sound. You will sit there and let me do my job. The best I can do for you is to get a reduced sentence."

"How reduced?" I was curious.

"Twenty years."

Knocker grinned. "Hey, mate. Fuck you."

Moments later, the judge appeared and the trial began. There were no witnesses, and I was the first to be questioned.

But before that, the judge went through formalities. And of course, he spoke rather good English.

"Mr. Kane, you are accused of the murder of General Mikhail Shatov, a decorated officer of the Russian military. How do you plead?"

"Not guilty."

The judge's eyebrows shot up. "Not guilty? Yet the evidence places you at the scene of the crime. How do you explain your presence at the hotel where General Shatov was killed?"

"Whoever told you that, Your Honor, is a liar. We weren't even at a hotel."

"We will see. Mr. Jensen, you are accused of the murder of General Mikhail Shatov, a decorated officer of the Russian military. How do you plead?"

"Not guilty by reason of insanity," Knocker replied.

"Here we go," I muttered to myself.

"Insanity, Mr. Jensen?"

"Yes, sir. You see, I'd been drinking a lot of beers, and I was quite hammered at the time. I didn't realize that she was your daughter."

There was a murmur from the press.

"What?"

"I said I didn't realize it was your daughter. Like I said, I was drunk, and it was possibly a good thing. She was fucking ugly."

A murmur rippled through the crowd, growing loud and ending in uproar. I couldn't help but grin.

"Silence! Mr. Jensen—"

"Her name was Olga, right?"

The judge's eyes blazed with fire. "I do not have a daughter named Olga."

"Sorry, my mistake. Was it your wife?"

"*Silence!*"

Knocker stopped.

The judge said, "Now, let's get started."

I was put in the witness box and the proceedings commenced.

The prosecutor was a military man, there was no hiding it. For the simple fact that he wore a uniform. He said, "You were seen in the same hotel, on the same floor, within minutes of the general's murder. That's an extraordinary coincidence, wouldn't you agree?"

"It would be if I was even there. Even more so if Shatov had been there too."

"You are denying it?"

"Yes."

The judge said, "Why was a man like you, an American, meeting with a Russian general at the very location of his death?"

"What location?"

"In the hotel?"

"I never met him in the hotel."

The prosecutor said, "You claim ignorance, yet security footage shows you entering the same hallway as Ivanov's suite shortly before the murder. How do you explain that?"

"It's doctored," I replied. "We met Shatov in Belarus."

"So, you admit to meeting him?"

"Yes."

"Then you did kill him."

"No," I replied.

The judge said, "What about the weapon? A knife, found in your room, matched the murder weapon exactly. How do you explain that?"

"Shatov was shot, not stabbed."

"So, you shot him."

"No, we didn't."

The prosecutor took over again. "So, you deny stabbing the general, but how is it you know that the general was shot?"

"We were there, we saw it happen. If you have a knife and are saying that the general was stabbed, then someone is lying."

"Who might that be?" the judge asked.

"Sergey Lash."

"Preposterous," the judge growled. "Where is your proof?"

"Don't have any."

The prosecutor looked at me before saying, "You say you were set up? Isn't it true that you and the general were well acquainted in political circles? You had differences of opinion, and that's why you killed him."

"If you mean we'd been trying to kill each other over the past few months then you'd be right. But when we met in Belarus, we met as men with a common cause."

"What cause might that be?"

"To bring down a crazy plot by Sergey Lash."

"You are saying that Mikhail Shatov met with you to plan an assault on the President of Russia? That would make him a traitor."

"Yes, I guess it would."

"Then I say that this is all lies. I say that you met with Mikhail Shatov in order to convince him to help you assassinate the president, and when he refused you killed him."

This guy was going all in. For a show trial, it was well rehearsed.

"No, that is not true."

"Witnesses say you threatened him during an argument. How do you respond to that?"

I smiled. "Are you on drugs?"

"What?"

"I mean, are you stoned? You must be because you haven't heard a word I've said."

"No more questions," the prosecutor said abruptly.

The judge nodded and I left the box. Then they made Knocker get in there, and a new circus began.

"Mr. Jensen—"

"Yes, Judge?" Knocker said, cutting him off.

"Do you agree with what your friend said?"

"No, sir."

"What do you see as different?"

"We were in Belarus at the time," Knocker said.

"That is what Mr. Kane said."

"Oh, sorry."

The prosecutor came out from behind his table. "Mr. Jensen, if you confess now, it would be better for you in the long run."

"Okay."

"So you are admitting that you killed General Mikhail Shatov?"

"No. I'm a habitual masturbator."

There was a snigger of laughter from the gallery.

The prosecutor turned red. "Making light of this trial will not help your situation?"

"Why? The whole thing is a joke."

"You think murder is a joke?"

"It wasn't murder," Knocker replied.

"Really? What was it?"

"An assassination performed by the Russian government to cover up the fact that Sergey Lash's wife was sleeping with a British national."

"What?"

"Shatov was going to come out with it on international television. Lash ordered his death to save face."

"Surely you can't be serious?" the prosecutor asked, aghast.

"Have you seen her? Whoa, she is a serious bit of crumpet that."

"How dare you insult the president's wife like that," the judge stormed.

Knocker nodded. "You're right, crumpet was a little harsh."

"Your Honor, I think we have heard enough," the prosecutor said.

"I agree. You have presented no credible defense. This court finds you guilty of the murder of General Mikhail Shatov. You will be sentenced to twenty years in a labor camp."

The gavel slammed down, bringing our sham trial to an abrupt conclusion. There was no need for a defense lawyer. I sure hoped he didn't expect us to pay.

"Take them away."

Placed in shackles once more, we were escorted from the courtroom. As we shuffled past the gallery, I caught sight of a familiar face with a press pass. The second part of our plan was about to commence.

"All hail Odin," I said in a soft voice.

Knocker glanced at me. "This is going to be bloody fun, Reaper."

CHAPTER 19

I SAID, "I'M GOING TO LET HOLLY TELL YOU THIS PART OF the story. After all, it is her story to tell."

"What do you mean?" German asked.

"While Knocker and I were banged up, Holly had put together another team to help with the next part of the operation."

Everyone in the room looked expectantly at Holly. German said, "All right, Miss Smith, let's hear what you have to say."

————

HOLLY

While John and Raymond were under the watchful eyes of our first team in Moscow, I had put together a second team consisting of Strike Team Krait to carry out a separate mission. We were about to take control of a gulag in the north of Russia above the Arctic Circle. Its name was Camp Death.

The Mi-35 helicopter was flying low through the snowstorm, the fates of all those aboard in the hands of the pilots who were bloody good at their job. After all, they were Russian and accustomed to flying in this kind of weather.

Boris Pushkin was responsible for supplying us with the fully crewed Mil Mi-35. When he was approached for his assistance, there'd been no hesitation whatsoever. Should our mission be successful, he would be elevated to the position of Russia's next president.

The roar of the Mi-35's engines cut through the storm, the vibrations thrumming through the floor beneath my boots. Snow whipped against the windows, thick flurries swallowed by the dark. The helicopter swayed in the gusts, but the pilot kept us steady, skimming low over the frozen wilderness. The Russian gulag appeared ahead, a hulking silhouette barely visible in the blizzard, like a shadow lurking in the storm but marked by only a few lights.

Upon finding out where John and Ray were being sent for incarceration, we went into action. Morozov was to be part of that escort as we had hoped. He was the ultimate target, and whether taken dead or alive was totally up to him. After that, we would go after Lash.

Inside my mask, my breath was steady, fogging up the glass just enough to remind me of the icy conditions waiting beyond the door. Surrounding me, the members of Strike Team Krait were silent, their faces obscured behind white camo gear. We were like phantoms in this storm, ghosts descending from the sky, our clothing designed to blend into the swirling white below.

Hovering just above the tree line, the helicopter's wheels barely brushed the tops of the pines as the doors opened and we dropped ropes to help us disembark.

The wind tore at the open doors as we slid down, dropping silently into the deep snow below. Hammond went first, followed by Kelly Morris. Then came the rest of us.

The downdraft from the rotors kicked up flurries, masking our descent as we hit the ground, crouching low in the frozen brush. I felt the frigid air bite through my gear. The Mi-35 banked away, disappearing once more into the storm, leaving us enveloped by the eerie quiet of the blizzard. The snow swallowed all sound.

We moved quickly, with Wombat Peters on point, spreading out through the trees as the gulag loomed closer. The first guard post came into view, a dark outline barely visible in the white chaos. Wombat signaled a sharp motion, and the team responded in silence. We crept forward, our movements in sync. The stormy conditions were fortuitous, our best ally, covering our approach, but there would be no second chances if we made a mistake.

A guard stood on the platform above, his silhouette shifting as he scanned the perimeter, unaware of the imminent threat. Beside me, Snake Lewis raised his suppressed Heckler and Koch 417 and sighted on the figure. He caressed the trigger, and the weapon fired.

The guard collapsed without a sound, his body crumpling to the floor of the tower. A perimeter guard had just turned when another suppressed shot hissed through the storm. He dropped, disappearing into the drifts, his lifeless form already blending into the landscape.

We moved swiftly to the fence and Hammond started to cut his way through. The storm still hid us from view. No alarms. No searchlights. Just the howl of the wind and the never-ending sweep of snow.

Kelly peeled the barbed wire back as Hammond cut. The Heckler and Koch I held in my hands swept the perimeter while they worked. Once the wire was cut enough, Hammond motioned again, and we slipped past the guard post and crouched in the shadows. The lights from the buildings flickered weakly, casting dim halos in the storm, but we stayed in the darkness.

"Everyone knows what they have to do?" I asked.

They responded quietly.

Two more guards patrolled near the main gate. Their figures were little more than faint shapes in the blizzard, trudging through the snow, their heads down against the wind. I watched Snake and Wombat close in on them before firing their weapons, any sound emitted whipped away in an instant. The guards dropped before they could react, their bodies falling limp into the drift.

With the gates secure, all we had to do now was take the rest of the camp.

Working our way toward the headquarters building, Kelly and I hopped in the shadows and utilized the buildings for cover. Once we reached the HQ building, Kelly and I waited. Hammond had gone after the camp's power source to shut it down.

"Krait One, sitrep?"

"Power source secure, Krait Five. Standby. All call signs standby to go dark."

Moments later, the camp lights went out and we pulled our NVGs down. I whispered two words into my comms, "Take them."

Kelly and I entered the HQ building, not loud, but certainly not quiet. The interior was dark, but thanks to our NVGs, we were fine.

Both the outer and main offices were clear. As we passed through the area, Kelly disabled the landlines. Behind the main office desk, we found another door, which was closed. I paused outside it and tried the knob. It turned and the door snicked open.

Pushing gently with my hand, it swung wider on oiled hinges and Kelly went through. Both of us swept the room beyond, our laser sights reaching out and touching everything we looked at. It was a living room. Bathed in darkness.

Using hand signals, Kelly directed me toward the door across the room. I hurried over and once again tried the knob. It too was open. I repeated my actions and pushed it wide.

Kelly passed through, and this time, I heard her suppressed weapon fire three times. I was only a couple steps behind her and swept my section of the room. At its center was a narrow bed. In it, now dead, was the commander of the gulag. I heard Kelly say, "Clear."

I said into my comms, "All call signs, Bear One is down."

Bear One was the name allocated for the commander. The others broke squelch, not willing to or couldn't talk at that moment.

Our next priority was the communications room. It was important to knock it out while the others were securing the rest of the gulag. For most facilities, it was nothing unusual for there to be up to a hundred soldiers on site at any one time. But because of the remote location of this gulag, there were only twenty. It would seem that there was little concern about escapes. To do so was to commit suicide. The only way out of the place was release or death. Most of the time, it was the latter.

We moved swiftly. The rest of the patrol guards were down, as were the ones in the watch towers. Reaching the communications room, we found a lone soldier inside, dispatching him swiftly.

Moments later, a call came over the comms. "Geronimo. I say again, Geronimo."

The barracks were secure.

"What do you mean secure?" Miriam asked.

I glanced at Holly.

"They were canceled as a threat," Holly replied.

"They were all killed?"

"Yes."

"How?"

"You don't want to know."

"Yes, I do."

"They were gassed with something called Intrepid 453."

"What the hell is Intrepid 453?"

"It's like a sleeping agent, except it shuts down every-thing once it takes effect. First comes sleep, then death. There is no pain involved with it."

Miriam seemed aghast at the thought of it. "Where did it come from?"

"It is a British invention."

"Why the hell don't I know about it?"

"You do now."

"Shit."

"Ma'am, when it comes to us, we're like a last resort. You are kept at arm's length so you have plausible deniability."

"So, you killed everyone there? Is that it?"

"All except the prisoners."

"Carry on. Fuck."

We left the prisoners locked up. There was nowhere they could go. Besides, we weren't there to free them. Our mission was Morozov and then Lash. They were the last two. With them gone, Pushkin could restore order to his country.

The storm continued to howl through the night, increasing the depth of the snow drifts. We called the Mi-35, which landed within the razor wire perimeter, enabling us to remain in contact with the outside world. By that, I mean Slick.

"You read me, boss?" he asked, sometime around three in the morning.

It was dark, and the snow was still falling. "I'm here, Alpha."

"The packages are on the way."

"Copy. Keep me updated."

"Roger that."

————

Ten minutes later, Hammond found me in the main office, standing next to a fire. He had Kelly with him. "Bloody cold out."

"Must be the weather," I replied.

He stared at me for a long moment. "You going to tell me what the aim of this mission is?"

"To free Kane and Knocker."

"Apart from that. There is something that doesn't add up."

"You knew that they were going to come here. How?"

"The subtle art of manipulation," Holly said. "And special effects."

"What do you mean?"

"ODIN."

"ODIN?"

"Yes. First, we replaced the judge. That was to make sure that they would be sent here. But even before that, we used special words that a psychologist recommended. We had ODIN in place within the Russian embassy in Paris, and whenever they came across Morozov, they used the words just in sentences. That planted the seed. It was the first time the psychological side was tried. It seemed to work."

Kelly nodded. "So they are being brought here, then what?"

"ODIN are now part of the escort. They will be with them all the way. As will Morozov because his arrogance won't let him do it any other way."

"How can they get away with it?"

"Because of the special effects people. Each one is impersonating a living person. Think Mission Impossible style disguises."

"What happens when they arrive?"

"The problem goes away," I replied.

"Away?"

"MI6 style."

"Okay, just as long as I know where we are."

"Once we're done here," I replied, "we're headed back to Moscow. One final mission."

"Lash?" he asked.

"Yes, Lash."

The helicopter with Kane and Jensen arrived at five. It was still dark, and the storm continued dumping snow. The pilot of the incoming reached out over the radio to get a weather report and was answered by one of Pushkin's pilots.

Ten minutes later, the helicopter touched down inside the wire. There was a flurry of movement as the doors opened and seven people alighted. They hurried toward the HQ, where we were waiting for them.

When the door crashed back, they all filed into the office. Kane and Jensen were looking fine. Morozov appeared angry. He stared at my back because I was facing away. The only other person in the room with me was Hammond.

"Are you going to acknowledge our arrival, Comrade?" he snarled at me.

I turned slowly and pulled back the hood on my coat so he could get a better look at me. "Hello, Genady."

"You!" He was surprised, to say the least. "What is this?"

I looked at one of the escorts. "Untie them."

"What is the meaning of this?"

"This is where justice prevails," I replied.

KANE

"I will take over now," I said. *"From here on out, you'll have a better understanding of what happened."*

The onset of angry buzzing in my pocket indicated that my cell was ringing. I took it out and said, "Almost there." I placed it back in my pocket before continuing.

While Morozov tried to work out what was happening, Knocker and I were freed from our bonds. All around us, our escorts removed their masks to reveal themselves. The only one missing from ODIN was Rose Holden. She'd remained behind in Moscow to lay the groundwork for the next part of our plan.

Morozov stared at me, knowing it was all over. "It would have given me great pleasure to see you die, Mr. Kane."

"You've lived long enough. Killed too many people, and if you'd had your way, killed a hell of a lot more."

"All for my country, just like you."

"I'm between countries at the moment," I replied.

"Pity there weren't more people like you in Russia."

"There is one thing I'm curious about," I said. "Why were you getting around Europe seeing all the exiled oligarchs? We assumed that it was to drum up support to oust Lash."

"Let's just say it is best to get before you are got," Morozov said with a wry smile.

I nodded my understanding.

"That would explain this," Holly said, passing over a piece of paper to the remaining general.

He read it and smiled dryly. "This was a one-way trip either way."

I glanced at Holly. She said, "Sometime before we arrived, a message came through to the commanding officer. It seems that Genady wasn't to be permitted to leave here."

Morozov stared at me. "I gather you will go after Sergey next?"

"That's right. He's the last, except for one. Hecate."

"I do not know who Hecate is. Only two people know. One of them is dead."

"Shatov?"

"Yes. The other is Sergey."

"I see."

"You will never get him out of the Kremlin," Morozov said.

"We'll see."

He shook his head. "It is impossible."

"Not with your help."

I glanced at Helen Smith from ODIN. She nodded. "I've got enough."

Morozov was confused. "What—"

That was as far as he got before I shot him.

CHAPTER 20

WE ALLOWED TWO DAYS TO ELAPSE BEFORE MOVING. BY then, the reports had come in regarding the deaths at the gulag and the fact that Morozov was nowhere to be found. We had seen to that, because we needed Lash to believe that the general was still alive.

Once we were ready, I made the call.

"Hello, Sergey," I said.

"Genady?"

ODIN had used their voice enhancement technology system to make me sound like Morozov when I spoke. "It is me, Sergey."

"What happened?"

"It was a clusterfuck."

"What?"

"I think someone is trying to kill me from within. I think you are the only one I can trust."

"Are you in Moscow?" Lash asked.

"Yes."

"Where?"

"I need to see you, Sergey. We have to plan for this. I think it is the oligarchs. They are trying to isolate us."

"You could be right," Lash lied. "We must work out what we are doing. Where will we meet?"

"Somewhere quiet, out of the way. Ivan's?"

Ivan's was a backstreet bar where people went when they didn't want to be seen. Lash said, "Yes, Ivan's."

"Tonight? At ten?"

"I will be there."

The call went dead, and our teams went to work.

We were all in position by nine. We had taken over the bar, with the help of Pushkin's people. I had been made up to look like Morozov while the rest of Groves's people were placed around the bar along with Holly, Knocker, and Slick. There were fifteen of us in all. We figured that was a good number because we knew Lash would bring a contingent with him.

I sat at a table with Holly and Helen Smith across from me. Helen was running through what I needed to do. "Once Lash is in position and you're ready, there is a button under the table. This will operate the charge strip that will hit him with enough of a charge to knock him out. It will also stop his heart, so should one of his men check him, they'll feel nothing and assume he's had a heart attack. That's when Ian comes in. Nothing like a doctor in the audience," she said with a grin.

She continued. "Within minutes, an ambulance will arrive, and you will ride with Lash. That's when we'll move on to phase two. By then, I will have injected Lash and his heart will be pumping again."

"Phase two, getting him out of Moscow."

"Yes. As soon as the vehicles arrive, they'll all be disabled. There is no chance of them following us."

"Providing all goes to plan," I said.

Helen nodded. "Yes."

But nothing ever goes to plan. Not all the way through.

Lash arrived on time and sat opposite me. His attendant guards spread around the bar. My disguise worked rather well because he never seemed to twig regarding my true identity. Thanks to the disguise and the voice technology.

"It is good to see you alive and well, Genady."

"I nearly wasn't," I replied.

"What happened?"

"The gulag was attacked. I managed to escape with a couple of men in the helicopter."

"Really? What happened to them?"

"I did not know who I could trust."

I left the rest unspoken, but he knew what I meant. "I see. The two men we sent there? Kane and Jensen?"

"Dead."

"So, what makes you think it is the oligarchs?"

"It has to be them. I heard whispers before I left that Pushkin was trying to rally them. That was why I was checking up on them before Paris."

"Pushkin?"

"Yes."

"Damn that man. We should have killed him when we had the chance."

"Yes."

"What do you suppose we do?"

I smiled. "I propose a holiday."

"What?"

"Maybe the UK."

"What are you on about?"

I pushed the button, and Lash died.

He slumped to the side. "Help. Someone help."

Lash's guards began milling around. Hammond appeared. "Get out of the way. I am a doctor."

Stepping in closer, he began checking the president over. "I can't find a pulse. Someone call an ambulance."

The barman went through the motions of faking a call, then called out, "It is on its way."

One of Lash's guards checked him. His head snapped up and he stared at Hammond. "What do we do?"

"Nothing. He is dead."

"But we must try."

"If the ambulance arrives in time, then he might have a chance."

Meanwhile, Lash's heart began beating again. While Hammond was checking, Helen, dressed as a civilian, had leaned down and injected Lash with something I'd never heard of before. All I know is that it got his heart working again.

A short time later, the ambulance arrived, and Lash was loaded onto it. I followed Hammond and the gurney out to the ambulance. Hammond climbed in, and one of the guards was about to follow him. I placed a hand on his shoulder to stop him. "I will go."

"No, it is my job."

My voice became sterner. "That is an order. Go back to the Kremlin and report what has happened."

"We will call it in."

"No, you fool. Who knows who will hear it. Maybe our enemies. Then where will we be? You must report it in person."

"Yes, Comrade General."

I climbed into the rear of the ambulance and the doors slammed behind me. I looked at Hammond and said, "Let's get the hell out of Moscow."

———

All of us took different routes. We dumped the ambulance at an underpass two miles from the bar, transferring into a black van. Hammond now drove while I was in the back with Helen Smith. I had ditched the mask I'd been wearing, enjoying the cool air on my own skin.

Helen checked Lash's vitals. "How is he?" I asked.

"Fine. Everything is normal."

"How long will he be out for?"

"The injection I gave him to start his heart also contained a new drug that will knock him out for a few hours. As long as we're in the air when he comes around, it'll be fine."

"You people are good at this," I said.

She smiled. "It's not all beer and skittles, as you Americans say."

"Coming up on the next changeover," Hammond called back.

I grabbed the Glock that I was now carrying and checked the loads. It was an old habit. I thrust it back into my belt and prepared to move. The van slowed and then came to a stop.

The doors were opened from the outside and standing there were Knocker, Holly, and Paul Cross. "About time you got here," Knocker said.

He helped me with Lash, and we loaded him into a blue van. "What happened after we left?"

"The guards had trouble with their vehicles as was planned. We all got out of there in our own rides. The others should be on their way to the airfield. That leaves just us."

With the second van loaded, we pulled away from the curb and started for the airfield where the Cessna Citation was waiting. There was one small hiccup, however, waiting along the way.

"We've got a tail," Cross called over his shoulder from the passenger seat in the van.

"What kind?" I asked.

"Black SUV."

"KGB?" I asked.

"How could they know?" Hammond asked.

"He's right," Knocker said.

I thought for a moment.

Then Cross said, "It was just joined by two more."

My mind whirled. Then, a puzzle piece fell into place, followed by more. "Son of a fucking bitch. Holly, get Pushkin on the phone."

"What?"

"Just do it," I said, pulling my Glock.

Knocker nodded slowly. "You figure this is Pushkin?"

"We're about to find out."

"I can't raise him," Holly said.

"Asked and answered," I muttered.

"Why would he do this after all the help we've given him?"

"Because he wants Lash, to put him on a pedestal. Then knock him off it. He's got what he wants from the west, now that he doesn't need us anymore, all bets are off."

"So, is he after Lash to put on trial or…"

"They want to kill him," Holly said. "Lash dies and they blame us. International incident and the Cold War that Lash started continues. Making Pushkin a big man."

"Here they come," Cross said. "Get ready."

Hammond put his foot down, making the van speed up, then took a hard left. He went into a narrow alley and sped toward the far end. I glanced at Helen. "Wake him up."

"What?"

"If we have to abandon this thing, I'm not carrying him. Wake him up."

She reached into her bag of tricks for a hypodermic and hit Lash with it. Moments later, he was conscious and we were approaching the end of the alley. I glanced over at Knocker. "You ready?"

"Does the pope have control of the Catholic church and—"

"Yes or no, idiot?"

"Yes."

"Stop the van!"

The van skidded to a stop. I threw open the rear doors and shouted as I climbed out, "Keep going. We'll see you at the plane."

The van sped off and Knocker and I stood in the

mouth of the alley, our weapons raised. The oncoming headlights preceded the roar of engines. I waited two more beats then said, "Fuck it."

The weapon in my hand bucked wildly as it hammered out round after round. Beside me, Knocker did the same. For a moment, I thought the lead vehicle was going to keep coming, but at the last moment, it swung hard left and hit the wall of a building. It sat there, blocking the alley.

"Press forward," I called to Knocker.

We moved toward the SUV. I grabbed the door and opened it, the light inside coming on to reveal a dead driver and mortally wounded passenger. The two SUVs behind had pulled up and doors were flung open and the men inside disembarked.

They opened fire and I felt like I'd been hit in the left shoulder with a hammer. I must have let out a yelp because Knocker turned to me and said, "Are you all right?"

"I'm fine," I lied as the burning lance of pain rocketed through my body.

We started to return fire, using the SUV containing the dead and dying as our cover. Another of Pushkin's men fell.

I could feel the blood running down my side. The throbbing pain was fast making my arm useless. I dropped out a spent magazine from the Glock and managed to reload. At my side, Knocker did the same.

I fired at a man who was shooting through a smashed side window. I could see his legs and fired again. A bullet took him in the knee, sending him sprawling to the ground, and I shot him once more. This time in the head, extinguishing his life.

By now, my arm was useless. Excruciating fire ran through my body and I was sweating like a summer's day. "Knocker."

"Yeah, Reaper?"

"You know when I said I was okay?"

Glancing at me, he quickly realized that I was sliding down the front guard of the SUV. "Ah, fuck."

He hurried to me to ensure I didn't go all the way down. "Don't do that, Mucker. I won't be able to get your ass back up."

I managed to get onto my knees. "Okay."

"Where are you hit?"

"Left shoulder."

"At least it wasn't your stupid head."

"Just another battle scar."

"Yeah."

I looked at him once he'd let off a few more rounds to hold the shooters at bay. I asked, "You got one?"

"Stupid fucking question," he said, digging into his pocket. He held up the frag grenade like it was an old friend. "You able to run?"

"Can barely bloody walk."

"You big sook."

"Shut up."

Knocker grabbed me by the collar and helped me to my feet in his most gentle manner. I moaned in pain, and he shoved me around the corner of the building. "Don't bloody move."

Then he turned back, pulled the pin, and tossed the grenade through the open door of the SUV. Then he stepped back to join me where I waited behind the building. "Hold on to your Tighty Whities."

The grenade detonated with a loud roar and orange flame exploded from the alley along with pieces of SUV. What it did, however, was create a roadblock that prevented the others from getting past. Knocker grabbed me and said, "Time to get out of here."

"How?" I asked.

He looked along the street and saw just the thing we needed. "We're going to take a cab."

The driver of the cab was far from happy, especially when Knocker did what he said we were going to do. We requisitioned the cab, leaving him on the side of the road. I was on the passenger side, bleeding all over his seat. Knocker glanced over at me and said, "You going to make it?"

"Flesh wound," I grunted.

"Black Knight shit, huh?" he said, referring to a Monty Python movie.

"Something like that."

―――――

It took another twenty minutes, but we made it to the plane. When we pulled up, Knocker called over to the others, "You'd better give me a hand."

"What's going on?" Holly asked.

"Reaper got shot. Lost a lot of blood."

By now, I was fading in and out of consciousness. Blood loss was well and truly kicking in.

"Damn it," Holly growled. "You two are just bloody—"

She threw her hands in the air as she ran toward the cab. Helen and Groves were close behind. Holly took one look and saw the amount of blood I'd lost and said, "Oh my God."

Once Groves and Knocker got me onto the plane, Helen began going over me, taking in the ashen color of my face and checking vitals. "We need to get some blood into him, or he'll die. What type?"

Holly shook her head. "No idea."

"Reaper, what blood type are you?"

"B."

"Are you sure?"

"Yes."

Helen looked back over her shoulder. "Rose, I need you."

"I'm here."

"Take a seat, I need your blood. When we're done with you, Chuck can fill in."

She took a seat beside me and rolled up her sleeve. Just before I blacked out completely, I said, "Lash?"

I never heard the answer.

———

That was how I got to Berlin alive. Two hits of blood and Helen watching over me. When I resurfaced two days later, the only ones around were Holly, Knocker, and Slick. The crew from ODIN were long gone. I never got to say thank you. Helen Smith—and the others—saved my life.

"*How long were you in the hospital for?*" German asked.

"*Ten days,*" I replied.

"*And you're fine now?*"

I nodded. "*A month later.*"

"What happened to Sergey Lash?" Christine Ryan asked. "Reports were that he died."

"That's what was said," I agreed.

"So, after you helped Pushkin, he tried to kill you? Is that it?" German asked.

"We thought so," I replied.

My cell buzzed. I checked it.

Holland said, "How any of you stay out of prison after this is beyond me."

"It's a good thing you won't be making that decision then, isn't it?" Miriam Craig said.

Holland pressed his lips together.

"I think we owe them a large debt of gratitude," Miriam continued. "I do have one question. You said you thought it was Pushkin who tried to kill you."

I nodded, but it was Holly who spoke. "It turned out that it was with someone's help."

"Who?" Anesha Perera asked.

"Hecate," Holly replied.

"You are still pushing that mole theory," German said. "But we are yet to see anything."

"We are close to finding out," Knocker said.

"How close?" asked Christine Ryan.

"This close," I replied, and on cue, the door opened, and three people walked in.

"Good grief," Holland said, aghast.

I glanced at German, who seemed frozen in shock. Christine Ryan, on the other hand, said, "President Lash, I see you are still alive."

Standing on either side of Lash were Hunt and Newman. I stood up from my seat. German finally found his voice. "But we were led to think that he was dead."

I nodded. "That's the way it was supposed to be.

Everyone currently in this room knew Sergey Lash was still alive except for you three."

"Why?" asked Holland.

"Because one of us is Hecate," Christine Ryan informed him.

"That would be correct," I said.

"Ridiculous," German said.

Holland came to his feet. "That is an abhorrent accusation."

"Sit down," Holly snapped.

I said, "We had our suspicions as to who it was. We just needed Sergey to confirm it."

"And?" Miriam Craig asked.

My stare fixed on Christine Ryan. "Everything pointed at Christine. In fact, we were convinced that it was her. Everything that went wrong was under her watch. Quite conveniently. Maybe even too convenient. Which was why we needed Sergey to confirm it."

"And did he?" Christine Ryan asked.

"You'll be pleased to know you are in the clear."

"As I should be."

I nodded. "Actually, there was one other person who wasn't privy to the facts of his survival. Sergey?"

"Miriam Craig."

Surprise lit her face. "What? I knew."

"No, you didn't," Knocker said. "We made sure you were kept out of it. When Sergey told us it was you, Slick looked into it, and guess what, you and Fergus Pridham were joined at the hip for a good while before he ran for PM. So, he dug deeper."

"Are you crazy, Raymond?"

"Quite fucking possibly. You see, while this was going on, you had people feeding you information from MI6, *including Christine Ryan, who had no idea what was really happening. Since you were part of the Intelligence and Security Committee of Parliament. What was the line she used, Christine?"*

"Keeping her finger on the pulse."

I said, "So, she knew everything that was happening. We were convinced it was Christine, but when we changed that and things still happened, there was still one common denominator. One we hadn't considered until Lash confirmed it."

"Wait," Miriam said. "What about when you went after Lash. I was kept out of that."

"Slick looked into that too. You talked to Pushkin just hours before the mission kicked off. My guess is to strike a deal with him. I don't know what about, but I'm guessing it will all come out in time. Maybe sanctions or getting NATO to pull back. Anyway, I don't care about that. Lash has made a full confession on tape."

"You are crazy!" Miriam shouted. "You will never get away with this. No one will take the word of a crazed killer."

"We'll let the courts sort through that," I said.

She glanced desperately at Knocker. "Raymond, you believe me, don't you?"

"Don't fucking call me Raymond."

The door opened again, and four MI6 security officers entered. They flanked Miriam and escorted her from the room. German stared at us. "So all this was staged for the benefit of smoking out a mole?"

I shrugged.

"Was any of it true?" Holland asked.

Holly said, "What we told you? Every word."

"The bomb?"

"Yes."

Anesha Perera came to my side. "We need to talk, John."

"Yes, but first I have to do something."

———

The Land Rover eased to a stop amid the mist-shrouded trees in the thick forest. The trees stood ramrod straight and disappeared into the curtain above. Two doors opened and Knocker and I climbed out. He said, "I'll get him."

I stared straight ahead at the trees. I heard the back door open and Knocker say something. Moments later, he and Sergey Lash were standing beside me. I took Lash by the arm and walked him forward around twenty paces. He stood looking straight ahead while I turned to face him side-on. My hand went to my belt and retrieved the Glock.

Somewhere in the trees, a nightingale chirped. I stared at Lash and raised the Glock so that it was mere inches from the side of his head. He said, "I wouldn't do it any differently."

"Yes," I said and then shot him.

A LOOK AT KANE: TOOTH & NAIL

BY MARK ALLENS WITH BRENT TOWNS

FROM THE AUTHOR OF THE TEAM REAPER SERIES COMES KANE.

When John 'Reaper' Kane is forced to gun down a fourteen-year-old boy in self-defense, the combat-weary warrior becomes disillusioned with the endless cycle of blood and violence his life has become.

Going off-grid in the remote mountain town of Vesper Lake for a week of soul-searching, he steps in to help a young woman, and his two-fisted interference finds him running afoul of the local sheriff. In the violent aftermath, he discovers that the town suffers under the crushing stranglehold of Nazareno 'The Nazarene Dragon' Pedregon, a ruthless drug lord commanding his criminal empire from inside Black Bog Federal Prison, a cesspool of death and corruption.

Framed for murder, Kane is dragged into the prison and forced to fight for his life when Nazareno finds out who he really is. Alone, exhausted, and outgunned, with enemies closing in on all sides, the odds are stacked against him. But when the hunt turns primal, Kane knows that the only way to survive is by tooth and nail.

AVAILABLE DECEMBER 2024

ABOUT THE AUTHOR

A relative newcomer to the world of writing, Brent Towns self-published his first book in 2015. Last Stand in Sanctuary took him two years to write. His first hardcover book, a Black Horse Western, was published the following year.

Since then, he has written twenty-six western stories, including some in collaboration with British western author, Ben Bridges; several action adventure novels, such as his bestselling Team Reaper series; the novelization to the 2019 movie, Bill Tilghman and the Outlaws; as well as scripted a handful of Commando Comics. Not bad for an Australian author, he thinks.

Often up until the small hours of the night, bashing away at his tortured keyboard in Queensland, Australia, Brent loves to lose himself in the world of fiction. If you're interested in sharing your thoughts in more detail, scan the QR code below! Your feedback is invaluable to him—and often helps shape his future writing endeavors.